Scott still couldn't believe the condition of the rooms inside Lisa's house.

"It's almost as if somebody has been watching the house," he said. "When I came by here last night to put the plywood in the window, everything was all right."

Fear flickered in Lisa's eyes. "I can't imagine why anybody would hate me enough to do so much damage. Yesterday I thought it was a burglar, but this is much more personal."

"Can you think of *anybody* who might be involved?" Scott asked.

He detected a slight tremor in Lisa's shoulders. She was trying to keep her fear from showing, but it was revealed in the frown that wrinkled her forehead.

She took a deep breath and raised her chin. "Aside from the guy already in jail, no. But it seems obvious that someone has a grudge against me."

Whoever was behind the burglaries at Lisa's house had to be stopped—and soon—before someone ended up getting hurt. Scott didn't want that someone to be Lisa.

Books by Sandra Robbins

Love Inspired Suspense

Final Warning
Mountain Peril
Yuletide Defender
Dangerous Reunion
Shattered Identity

SANDRA ROBBINS,

a former teacher and principal in the Tennessee public schools, is a full-time writer for the Christian market. She is married to her college sweetheart, and they have four children and five grandchildren. As a child, Sandra accepted Jesus as her Savior and has depended on Him to guide her throughout her life.

While working as a principal, Sandra came in contact with many individuals who were so burdened with problems that they found it difficult to function in their everyday lives. Her writing ministry grew out of the need for hope that she saw in the lives of those around her.

It is her prayer that God will use her words to plant seeds of hope in the lives of her readers. Her greatest desire is that many will come to know the peace she draws from her life verse, Isaiah 40:31—*But those who hope in the Lord will renew their strength. They will soar on wings like eagles, they will run and not grow weary, they will walk and not be faint.*

SHATTERED IDENTITY

SANDRA ROBBINS

Love Inspired

Recycling programs
for this product may
not exist in your area.

LOVE INSPIRED BOOKS

ISBN-13: 978-0-373-67500-5

SHATTERED IDENTITY

www.LoveInspiredBooks.com

Printed in U.S.A.

And He said unto me,
My grace is sufficient for thee:
for my strength is made perfect in weakness. Most
gladly therefore will I rather glory in my infirmities,
that the power of Christ may rest upon me.
—*2 Corinthians* 12:9

To the brave men and women who leave their homes and families to risk their lives by serving in the United States military. The personal sacrifices they endure provide all Americans a model of selfless devotion to the preservation of our country.

A very special thanks goes to Master Sergeant Tim Hardy, who allowed me to use his true experience with a lamb on a dusty road in a faraway country.

ONE

A sliding sound followed by a thump echoed through the darkened house.

Lisa Wade set her purse and two bags of groceries onto the kitchen table and listened. Was that a drawer closing? She tensed and listened for the sound to repeat, but the only thing she heard was the beating of her heart.

Someone's in the house.

She dismissed the thought as soon as it popped into her head. Her imagination was playing tricks on her. If there'd been any indication of forced entry when she had come in the back door, she would have noticed. After all, working as a dispatcher at the Ocracoke Island Sheriff's Office for three years had taught her to be observant of her surroundings.

A question flashed in her mind. What if she had overlooked something? She was distracted when she'd arrived home. The renovations of her house had occupied her mind all day, and she'd thought of little else.

She glanced at her watch. 6:00 p.m. Scott Michaels, the new deputy, had just come on duty for night patrol. He could be here within minutes and check out the house. She reached in her purse for her cell phone but drew her hand back. Even though Scott seemed like a nice guy, she didn't know him well. There was no need to give him, a former military officer, the impression she was a helpless female.

Ignoring the thoughts pounding in her head of what she should do, she glanced around the kitchen. Her breakfast dishes still sat in the sink, and the box holding the new kitchen wallpaper was on the table where she'd placed it last night. The kitchen looked as she had left it, although with her renovation in progress it was hard to tell. She stepped around two buckets of wall paint and tiptoed across the linoleum-covered floor. Her footsteps echoed like a pounding bass drum in the house.

As she moved through the dining room and into the living room, she mentally chided herself. What was there to be afraid of? After all, there hadn't been a home burglary on Ocracoke in months. And if a burglar wanted something of value, he'd choose one of the high-priced condos or vacation homes on the island, not a small bungalow that looked as though it had seen better days.

The evening light cast a flickering pattern across the worn carpet that had been on the living room floor ever since Lisa could remember. A stool lay on its side next to the stone fireplace, and she bent over to set it upright.

Another slide and thump from the direction of the bedroom sliced through the stillness in the house, and her heart leapt into her throat. She straightened and opened her mouth, but no sound came from her throat. She swallowed and tried again. "Wh-who's th-there?"

Silence.

The sound she'd heard had nothing to do with imagination. *Get out of the house now,* her mind screamed. She wanted to run, but fear rooted her feet to the floor.

Her eyes widened at the sight of a ghostly shadow looming across the carpet. It mingled with the dancing sunray patterns on the floor as it approached from behind.

"What…"

Before she could turn, her head exploded in a burst of pain. She grabbed at her head and staggered. She'd been struck. Her legs wobbled, and waves of dizziness washed over her. If she could make it to the front door, maybe she could escape. She shook her head to clear her blurred vision but groaned at the searing pain that flashed in her head like a burst of light.

Clawing at empty air to steady herself, she closed her eyes and toppled forward. With a thud she sprawled facedown on the floor, the impact knocking the breath from her body. Instinct warned her not to move even though she realized her attacker stood beside her. Through the narrow slit of her eyelids, she saw a hand descend as if in slow motion. It drifted downward and lifted her limp arm. Something tugged at her finger, and her grandmother's ring slid over her knuckle.

"Noooo," she moaned.

The sound of running footsteps penetrated the fog in her mind, and she heard a door close. She tried to push up, but her arms collapsed. Unable to move, Lisa gasped for breath as a kaleidoscope of brightly colored patterns flashed through her head. Her body relaxed, and she welcomed the darkness drifting into her mind. Her last conscious thoughts were of the rough carpet scratching her cheek and her grandmother's ring that had been passed down in their family for five generations.

Deputy Scott Michaels drove his squad car along the main road that twisted through Ocracoke Village. He liked this time of day, when the sidewalks weren't as crowded as they were earlier. With the summer tourist season in full swing, most visitors were getting ready for a relaxing dinner after spending a long day at the beach. Soon long lines would crowd the restaurants and wisps of smoke would curl upward from grills on the decks of condos and vacation rentals scattered throughout the village.

In the year since he'd come to live on Ocracoke Island, the small barrier island twenty-five miles off the coast of North Carolina, he'd settled in to island life and his new job as a deputy for the Hyde County Sheriff's Department. He wondered, however, if the island residents would ever really think of him as an O'cocker, as the locals called themselves.

This was the last shift for his rotation on night patrol, and he was glad. He liked the activity of the daytime when the road through town was crowded with bicycles and families enjoying their short time on the island. Nighttime patrol consisted of checking the bars and beaches for tourists who'd had too much to drink and testing the doors of businesses to make sure they were locked.

As he approached the village boundary, he spied the turnoff for Oyster Road. Lisa Wade, the pretty dispatcher at the office, lived at the end of the road in an old house she'd inherited when her grandmother died a few months ago. He'd never told her when he was on night patrol he would drive down to check out her house. She'd probably think it was crazy, but he felt uneasy with an attractive woman living alone in such a deserted area.

His sister Kate had suggested several times he ask Lisa out. No way was that going to happen. At the turnoff, he slowed and debated if he should drive down to her house. Maybe he should head on out to the beach.

Almost against his will, he turned onto the road and drove to the dead end where her house stood, next to a dune ridge that bordered a small section of beach. The remote location seemed to agree with Lisa until recently, when she'd announced she was going to renovate the house, put it up for sale, and leave the island.

Now as he approached, he studied the small bungalow. The frame house with its shutters and wicker chairs on the front porch looked like many other homes that had withstood the forces of nature in the past on Ocracoke. Fig trees sprouted from the sandy soil and dotted the front yard. Oyster shells scattered at their bases completed the picture of a typical island dwelling.

Lisa's car, the back door on the driver's side open, sat in the driveway next to the house. Scott frowned. Why would Lisa leave the car door ajar? Before he realized it, he had turned into the driveway and stopped behind her automobile.

When he stepped up to the open door, he smiled in understanding. Three sacks of groceries sat in the car's rear seat. She must have left those while she took others inside. He reached into the vehicle and pulled the bags out. He'd take them to the door and save her another trip outside.

He rounded the side of the house, stepped onto the back porch and knocked. "Lisa. It's Scott Michaels. I have the rest of your groceries."

Several seconds passed with no answer. He knocked again. When she didn't respond, he turned the knob. Locked.

The skin on the back of his neck prickled just as it had every time he'd encountered a dangerous situation in the military. His uncanny sixth sense told him something wasn't right. Lisa wouldn't lock herself in her house with three sacks of groceries still outside. He moved to the window by the swing and peered inside but could see nothing in the dark house.

Alarmed now, he dashed down the steps and around the house onto the front porch. He shook the handle of the locked front door and pounded his fist against it. "Lisa! Answer me. Are you in there?"

With no answer, he ran to the window behind the wicker chairs and squinted through the pane. His heart thudded when he caught sight of Lisa lying on the living room floor.

He turned his mouth to his lapel mike. "EMS needed at 100 Oyster Road."

"Ten-four." The answer crackled on the still air.

Scott picked up one of the chairs, crashed it against the window, and hammered at the glass until it lay splintered into pieces. Then he climbed through the opening and knelt beside Lisa's still form. Blood trickled down the side of her face.

"Lisa! Can you hear me?"

There was no response. His gaze raked her still form. He groaned and fought the déjà vu settling over him. It was always the same. He closed his eyes, and attempted to block the pictures forming in his mind. It was no use. Perspiration beaded his forehead, and his heart rate accelerated.

The memory of another time and another place seared his brain. Exploding mortar shells pounded inside his head, and distant cries for help echoed above the deadly noise. He rocked back on his heels, clutched the arm of the wounded man on the ground, and turned his face to the sky.

"Medic!" he screamed.

The sound bounced off the walls and brought him back to reality. His breath caught in his throat, and his eyes blinked open. He stared at the person on the floor next to him. This wasn't a soldier, not one of his men. This was Lisa Wade, the dispatcher from the station. His fingers relaxed on her arm, and he swallowed the nausea rising in his throat.

Sirens wailed in the distance. In an effort to shake the images of the past from his head, he gulped several deep breaths of air before he jumped to his feet and ran to open the front door. The Ocracoke ambulance screeched to a stop in the front yard. Two EMTs jumped out and ran to the porch.

"In here," Scott yelled.

The men pushed past him into the living room and knelt beside Lisa. They had their emergency bags open by the time they were on their knees. One glanced up. "What happened?"

Still shaken, Scott struggled to speak. "I—I don't know. I couldn't get her to the door. When I looked in the window, I saw her lying on the floor in front of the fireplace. There's blood on her forehead."

Unable to watch the men work, he eased down the steps into the yard. He raised a trembling hand to his forehead and wiped at the perspiration that dotted his brow. Would his nightmare ever be over? At times he thought so, but then some event sent his mind spiraling into combat memories he'd tried to erase.

The doctors in San Antonio had told him he would have recurring flashbacks to his battle experiences, and they were right. He raked his hand through his hair and took several more deep breaths. If he reacted this way every time he faced an emergency situation, perhaps taking a job as deputy had not been the best idea.

He walked to his cruiser and leaned against the fender. Burying his face in his hands, he whispered the words he'd come to rely on to take away his memories. "Remember the lamb."

Repeating the phrase over and over, he strode back and forth across the front yard while the EMTs continued their work. Within minutes his heart rate slowed, and the flashback he'd withstood in the house receded from his mind.

He shifted the focus of his thoughts to questions about Lisa. What could have happened after she came home that left her lying unconscious in a locked house? And why were groceries still in her car?

Maybe she had fallen, but he didn't see anything she could have hit her head on. Scott glanced at the house and swallowed the fear that rose in his throat. She had to be all right. She was part of the team he worked with now, and he didn't think he could face adding one more casualty to the list. He lifted his eyes toward heaven and said a prayer for her life.

"Deputy Michaels." One of the EMTs stood in the open front door and motioned for him.

"What is it?"

"She's coming around. She's got a nasty bump on her head, and her oxygen level is low. We're going to transport her to the health center."

Scott walked back into the house and stared at Lisa's pale face. An oxygen mask covered her mouth and nose. Her eyelids blinked open, and the scared look in her blue eyes pierced his heart. He knelt beside her and took her hand. "You're all right now, Lisa." He glanced over his shoulder at the broken window. "I wish I could say the same for your house, but don't worry about the window. I'll fix it later. Right now we're going to take you to the health center. I'll follow the ambulance. Is there anyone you'd like for me to call?"

She gave an almost imperceptible shake of her head. "W-wait a-a wh-while."

He nodded. "Okay. I'll stay with you."

She squeezed his hand and smiled. "Thank you."

One of the EMTs put his hand on Scott's shoulder. "Let's get this young lady loaded and on her way."

Scott moved out of the way and watched the men load Lisa in the ambulance. On the drive to the health center, he replayed the events in his mind, but they still made no sense. When they pulled into the driveway at the Island Health Center, he breathed a sigh of relief at the sight of Doc Hunter's battered truck in the parking lot. The man possessed medical knowledge and skills unlike any Scott had encountered before.

Thirty minutes later, Scott stopped pacing across the waiting room floor when the doctor walked into the room. Doc Hunter peered over the top of the wire-rimmed glasses on his nose. "Well, our girl has a bad bump on her head and a mild concussion, but I think she's going to be all right."

"Good. What about the blood on her forehead?"

"That's from the small cut caused by whatever she was struck with, but it'll heal without sutures."

"Struck with?" Scott's eyes widened. "So she was attacked by someone?"

Doc Hunter nodded. "That's what she says. Evidently she walked in on a burglar. It's a good thing you dropped by when you did. Her house is in such a deserted place, she could have lain there all night without anyone finding her."

For the first time since catching sight of her on the floor, Scott relaxed. "Is she really going to be all right?"

"I think she'll be fine, but I want to keep her tonight for observation. If all goes well, she'll be able to go home in the morning. But I'll keep a close watch on her for the next few weeks to make sure she doesn't have any problems with vision or coordination."

Scott looked past the doctor, down the hallway to the examining rooms. "Do you have someone to stay with her tonight?"

"Yes. I have a nurse who comes in when we have overnight patients. But Lisa's asking to see you now. She's in the third room on the right."

Scott smiled and stuck out his hand. "I appreciate all you've done for her. Thanks for taking care of her, Doc."

The doctor shook his hand and chuckled. "I've

been taking care of everybody on this island for a lot of years. Now, go on and see her."

Taking a deep breath, Scott walked down the hallway and stopped at the door of Lisa's room.

"Come in." Her soft voice was barely audible.

He stepped into the room and froze where he stood. Tremors shook his body, and scenes he'd tried to forget flashed through his mind like rocket fire on a dark night. It wasn't the hospital gown she wore, the bed where she lay or the bandage at the top of her forehead that stunned him, but the sight of the two prongs in her nose and the tube running oxygen to them. A nasal cannula—the medic at the base had called it. How many men had he seen gasping for breath as those tubes tried to pump oxygen into a dying soldier? He covered his eyes with his hand and groaned.

"Scott, are you all right?"

He opened his eyes and blinked. Lisa had pushed up on her elbows, and a panic-stricken look lined her face. *Remember the lamb.* He tried to smile, but his lips wouldn't cooperate.

"I—I'm fine. How are you feeling?"

She relaxed and lay back in the bed. "My head hurts, but Doc says I'll be fine. I understand I have you to thank for finding me."

He waved his hand in dismissal and grinned. "Just doing my job, ma'am." He hoped she didn't notice how his voice shook. A smile pulled at her lips, and his heart pounded. He'd never noticed how her blue eyes crinkled at the corners when she smiled. She really was a beautiful young woman. He pulled his thoughts back to the business at hand. "But tell me what happened."

As she related the story, his concern grew. When she finished, she held up her right hand and stared at it. Tears rolled down her cheeks. "He took my grandmother's ring off my finger. The day she gave it to me she said she hoped I would love it as much as she did. It belonged to her grandmother. And now it's gone."

Scott searched his mind for some words that might comfort Lisa, but he couldn't think of anything. "I'm so sorry, Lisa. Maybe we'll recover it."

She wiped her eyes on the corner of the sheet and shook her head. "You're forgetting I work at the sheriff's office. I know what the odds are that I will ever see my ring again."

"We'll try to find out who did this, Lisa. What about enemies? Is there anyone you've had problems with lately?"

"No, not that I can recall. But who knows what people who've been arrested think when they pass through our office? Maybe I made someone angry there."

He nodded. "It's a possibility. But for now, do what the doctor says. I'll come by in the morning.

In the meantime, if you think of anything, call me. I'll be on patrol all night."

"I will, and thank you again, Scott."

She held out her hand, and he grasped it. She covered his fingers with her other hand, and his skin burned from her touch. The scent of her perfume filled his nostrils, and he inhaled the fruity smell. The warm rush of emotion that coursed through his veins turned to ice at a chilling thought. Lisa could be the one—the woman he'd prayed he would never meet.

He'd known it since his first day on the job, and it scared him. For both their sakes, he needed to keep his distance. He pulled free of her grasp.

A questioning look crossed her face. "Is something wrong?"

He frowned and shook his head. "I need to get back on patrol. I'll see you in the morning."

He turned and hurried from the room. Back in the parking lot, he climbed in his squad car and gripped the steering wheel. What had happened to him just then? One moment he was questioning Lisa about her attacker and the next he was experiencing emotions he thought he'd long laid to rest. He had vowed he would never become involved with a woman. Not when he knew there was no future in it. There could be none, after all he'd seen and done.

How many assignments had there been through

the years? He didn't know. He'd lost count long ago, but they'd taken their toll. His buddies might have been able to come home and pick up their lives with wives and children, but he couldn't. Now he found himself attracted to a woman he worked with every day, but he would never act on those feelings.

Lisa Wade was too nice a person to be exposed to the nightmare of his life.

TWO

Most mornings after coming off all night on patrol Scott couldn't wait to get home, have something to eat and fall into bed. Not today. One minute the thought niggled at his mind that he should go check on Lisa, and then every reason why he should stay away popped into his head. He never would have believed a pretty blonde with the biggest blue eyes he'd ever seen could produce such conflicting emotions in his soul.

Shaking his head to clear his thoughts, he clutched Lisa's purse in one hand, and trudged down the hallway of the Island Health Center. The door to her room stood ajar, and he stopped to knock. A man's voice drifted from inside.

"Why didn't you call me last night after you were brought in? I would have been here with you. You know how much I love you."

Surprise, mingled with a grudging disappointment, set his pulse to racing. He'd never considered Lisa might be involved with someone, but it was for the best. Right now he needed to get out of here. He took a step to leave when a nurse exited a room at the end of the hall.

"May I help you?" She held a breakfast tray and smiled as she walked toward him.

He glanced down at Lisa's purse. "I'm the officer who found Miss Wade yesterday. I've brought her purse."

The woman's smile grew bigger. "I'm Kathy Prescott. I work nights when Doc Hunter needs a patient watched. I'm taking Lisa some breakfast. Come on in with me."

Scott held out the bag and backed away. "I don't want to bother her during breakfast. You can just give it to her."

Nurse Prescott juggled the tray in one hand and pushed the door open with the other. "I'm sure she'd like to see you. Come on in." The door swung open, and she walked into the room. "You have another visitor."

"Oh, who is it?" Lisa's voice drifted into the hall.

"The officer who found you yesterday."

"Scott?" Lisa called out. "Is that you? Come on in."

Taking a deep breath, Scott forced a smile to his face and stepped into the room. The nurse set the tray on a table beside the bed. "I'm going to leave this for you. If you need any help, let me know."

Lisa shook her head. "I'll be fine. Thank you, Kathy."

He stopped at the end of the bed and nodded to the nurse as she brushed past him. When she'd disappeared out the door, he held out Lisa's purse. "I went by your house last night to put some plywood on the window. Your groceries were still in the bags in the kitchen, and I put them away. I saw your purse on the table beside them. I thought you might need it."

"How kind of you." She pointed to the bedside table. "Just put it there. It's good to see you this morning."

He set the purse on the table next to her breakfast tray and darted a glance at the man standing on the other side of the bed. His heart dropped to the pit of his stomach. It was clear what Lisa saw in this man. With his rugged appearance, he could very well have been on the cover of any of the outdoor magazines on the rack at the Island General Store.

The cargo shorts and T-shirt he wore made Scott think this guy, even though he appeared to be in his late twenties, could fit right in with the college students who flocked to their beaches in the summer. His dark hair tumbled over his forehead, and a day's growth of beard that shadowed his face gave him a scruffy look.

Scott pulled his gaze away from the man and back to Lisa. Even in a hospital gown she had a glow about her this morning. He wondered if it was because of her visitor. Scott tried to act casual. "How're you feeling today?"

"I'm fine." Her eyes sparkled, and she glanced at the man beside her. "Scott, I'd like for you to meet my cousin Jeff Wade. He came by to check on me." She turned to Jeff. "And this is Scott Michaels, the man who found me unconscious yesterday."

"Cousin?" Scott tried to ignore the relief that washed over him.

Jeff came around the bed and stuck out his hand. "Yeah. My dad and Lisa's were brothers."

Scott grasped Jeff's hand. "I'm new to Ocracoke, so I don't know all the family connections yet."

"There's not much to learn about our family. Lisa and I were both only children, and our parents are dead. We lost our grandmother a few months ago, so Lisa and I are the only ones left." He paused. "And she's about to leave me by myself on Ocracoke."

Lisa sighed and repositioned the pillow behind her back. "We've been over this a dozen times, Jeff. We'll stay in touch."

"I know. I guess I'm trying to make you want to stay." He glanced at his watch. "I didn't realize it's getting so late. I need to get to work."

A small frown creased Lisa's forehead. "How are things going at the lighthouse?"

"Fine. Of course it's just part-time, and it's mostly maintenance-type stuff. But I did get another part-time job with Travis Fleming." Jeff shrugged. "I'm mostly a gofer for him. Last week I took one of his boats to the mainland to get it worked on, and I'll go over to bring it back in a few days."

Lisa's frown turned to a smile. "Good for you. I'm glad things are working out for you. Travis is a nice guy. Maybe your job with him will turn into something better."

"I hope so. But enough about me… Are you sure you don't want me to stay with you for a few days?"

Lisa shook her head. "No, I'll be fine. Now, go on. Don't be late."

Jeff shook his head. "Lisa, I wish you'd listen to me. Until the police find out who attacked you yesterday, you don't need to stay by yourself. Grandma's house is too isolated." He inclined his head toward Scott. "I hate to think how long you could have been there if Deputy Michaels hadn't come by."

"You're being overprotective as always, Jeff. I'm sure this was a random burglary. Whoever did it is probably already on the mainland by now."

Jeff scowled and let out a ragged breath as he

turned to Scott. "She's too quick to dismiss this incident. There may be more to this than she's willing to admit. Can't you persuade her to at least check into a motel or stay with friends until this guy is caught?"

Scott tensed at the concern flickering in Jeff's eyes. "You sound as if you think Lisa might be the target of someone with a grudge. Is that possible?"

Jeff's eyebrows arched, and he glanced at Lisa. "Doesn't he know?"

Lisa pushed up in bed and shook her head. "Scott is new to the island. There's no reason he should know."

"Know what?" He took a step closer. "Lisa, is there something you're not telling me that might help catch this guy?"

Her face turned crimson, and she clutched the top of the sheet covering her. "It's personal, Scott. I don't want to talk about it."

A long sigh escaped Jeff's lips. "I'm sorry, Lisa, but I think it's something he needs to know." He turned toward Scott. "A year ago there was a deputy on the island who was arrested and sent to prison for being involved in a burglary ring on the mainland."

Scott nodded. "I know about that. Calvin Jamison was the deputy. I took his job."

"What you may not know is that he was a ladies' man. He almost had a hypnotic effect on women, and Lisa was no exception. He thought he had her under his spell, but it turned out she was the one who discovered where he met up with his buddies on the mainland. He's in prison now, and he blames Lisa for not protecting him."

"Is this true?" Scott stared at Lisa.

"Yes."

"How do you know he blames you?" he asked.

"He's written me several times from prison. In his letters he says he still has friends on the outside, and I should be careful."

Scott's heart hammered in his chest. "Is that why you want to leave the island?"

She nodded. "That's one reason. There are others...."

Jeff returned to her bedside. "I just want you to be safe, Lisa. Who knows what Calvin is capable of? If one of his friends attacked you, they may very well do it again."

"Jeff's right, Lisa. This is information we needed to know." He glanced back at her cousin. "Thanks for telling me."

"I knew Lisa wouldn't, and I thought this information might be helpful." He glanced at his watch again before he leaned over and kissed Lisa on the forehead. "I really have to go now. If you change your mind about me staying with you, let me know."

"I will."

When Jeff left, Scott searched his mind for the right words to say to Lisa. He stuck his hands in his pockets and rocked back on his heels. "I'm sorry if you were embarrassed by what your cousin told me, but I think it'll be helpful in our investigation."

She pushed her long blond hair away from her face. "Jeff made it sound much worse than it really was. I didn't date Calvin, although I wanted to. He strung me along with promises, but he never intended to follow through on anything. He was using me just like he did everybody else he knew."

"Has he really threatened you since he's been in prison?"

Lisa shrugged. "It's been more like reminders of what he can do. He's written me several letters. In them he'll say things like he knows what a deserted spot my house is in, and how I should look over my shoulder all the time." She took a deep breath. "He's angry with me because I told the sheriff about a telephone conversation I overheard him having with someone on the mainland. That's where the deputies found his accomplices and arrested them."

She sat up straighter in the bed and drew the sheet up to her chin. His heart raced at how vulnerable she looked lying in the hospital bed. Like him, she'd had some experiences in her past that had left scars. He didn't like to dwell on his, and she probably didn't want to focus on hers, either.

Perhaps he should change the subject. There would be time later to discuss Calvin and any threats he had made. He smiled and glanced at the tray on the table. "Do you need some help with your breakfast?"

"No. I'm not very hungry this morning. I just want my coffee right now."

Scott picked up the cup and handed it to her. "Cream and sugar?"

"Black's fine." She took a sip, and her shoulders relaxed. "I needed this. Dealing with Jeff under the best of circumstances can be challenging."

Her words surprised Scott. He pulled a chair to the side of the bed and sat down. "What do you mean?"

Lisa leaned against the pillows at her back and held the coffee cup with both hands in front of her. "Jeff has had a lot of problems in his life, but he seems to be on the right track now. If I didn't think so, I couldn't leave the island."

Scott wanted to question her further, but it was none of his business. He exhaled deeply. "He may have problems, but the things he said concern me. I talked to my sister Kate this morning. She wants you to stay with her for a couple of days."

Lisa nodded. "I know—she called. But I hate to impose on her like that. She's getting ready for the baby. I really just want to go home."

"I don't think that's a good idea. Especially after what I've heard this morning."

She took a sip from her cup. "I've thought about what happened yesterday, and unlike Jeff I've come to the conclusion that Calvin had nothing to do with it."

"What makes you think so?"

"I came to know Calvin quite well when he worked as a deputy. He likes to make people think he's strong and in control all the time, but I really think he's scared now that he's in prison. He wants to get back at me, to make me as scared as he is. But it's not going to work."

"If it wasn't a friend of Calvin's, then who was it?"

She shook her head. "I don't know. I think I probably interrupted a burglar who panicked after I arrived home, and he hit me on the head to give him time to get away. I can't let this scare me and keep me from continuing with what I've already started. I'm leaving this island for good as soon as I finish renovating and selling my house."

"But…"

She sat up straight in the bed. "My mind is made up, Scott. I'm going back home this afternoon. Even though Kate is on maternity leave from her deputy's job, she's going to fill in for me today at the station. I think by tomorrow I'll be able to be back at dispatch."

The tone of her voice rang with determination. Although he wished he could make her see reason, Scott realized there was nothing he could do to change her mind. "Then at least let me change the locks for you."

She chuckled. "As if that would keep an intruder out. You know as well as I do there are videos all over the internet that show how to unlock a door. I saw one the other day that used the clip of a ball-point pen. I'll be more careful in the future and be more aware of my surroundings."

Scott raised his hands in resignation. "Have it your way, but I didn't know you were such a stubborn woman."

She arched her eyebrows and brushed her hair over her shoulder. "Not stubborn. Independent. Even though my grandmother raised me, I feel like I've been on my own all my life. She was sick most of the time, and I ended up taking care of her more than she did of me."

"At least you had somebody."

Lisa bit down on her lip and nodded. "I don't want to appear like I'm prying into your personal life, but everybody on the island knows your story."

Scott's heartbeat quickened as the story the island had talked about for the past year replayed in his mind. He wondered what life would have been like if his mother had lived when he was born. How different would he be if his father had raised him? Instead he'd been kidnapped by his mother's sister and reared to think he had no other family.

When the anger against his aunt overcame him, he tried to counteract it by thanking God that even until his death his father had never quit looking for him. Then his half sisters, Kate, Betsy and Emma, had continued the quest until a private investigator had finally found him after he'd been released from a military hospital in San Antonio a year ago. Now he was on Ocracoke Island with his family, living where he should have been all along.

"I lost a lot of years with my family," he muttered.

Lisa pushed up straighter in bed. "But you're here now, and I've never seen Kate and Betsy so happy."

He chuckled and stood. "And don't forget Emma. That eleven-year-old sister of mine has kept me on my toes ever since I came to Ocracoke. She's quite a girl."

At the mention of Emma, Lisa smiled. "Emma and her cat are favorites of everybody on the island. I'm glad you're going to be able to see her grow into a woman."

"Me, too." He stifled a yawn and glanced at his watch. "I think my night is catching up with me. I need to go home and get to bed. If you'll call me when Doc discharges you, I'll drive you home."

"Really, Scott, you've done enough."

He backed toward the door. "You know my cell phone number. Give me a call when you're ready to go, and I'll come get you."

She smiled gratefully. "Thanks for offering."

He snapped a salute in her direction and grinned. "The Ocracoke deputies aim to please, ma'am. Glad I could be of assistance."

Her laughter followed him into the hall. He closed the door, leaned against the wall for a moment and let the smile he'd pasted on his face dissolve. His stomach felt as if it was twisted in knots, but he thought he'd kept his tension well hidden. After seeing her this morning, he felt more confused than before. Ever since his visit yesterday he'd tried to convince himself he'd only felt the attraction to Lisa because he'd let down his guard. Now he wasn't so sure.

The twinge of jealousy he'd felt when he heard a man's voice in Lisa's room and the relief he was her cousin had shocked him. He couldn't let himself dwell too much on the way her smile stirred his heart. She was going to leave the island, and to his way of thinking she couldn't go soon enough.

Lisa lay back on the pillows and thought about the brooding man who'd just left her room. Kate, her best friend and Scott's half sister, had introduced them soon after he'd arrived on the island a little over a year ago. During that time, he had kept to himself a lot, and she had only gotten to know him better since he'd joined the force a few months ago.

As it did every time she thought about the new deputies in Ocracoke, guilt washed over her. Thoughts of Doug O'Neil, the young deputy who'd died in the line of duty a year ago, filled her mind. She shut her eyes in an effort to banish the painful memories, but it was no use. There was no escaping the remorse she felt for snubbing Doug when he showed an interest in her. Instead, she had her sights set on Calvin, who'd sweet-talked her just as he had every other woman on the island.

The guilt she felt turned to anger. She'd always thought of herself as an intelligent person, but she hadn't been able to see through Calvin's lies and deceptions. The worst part was she'd told herself her feelings for him were love. How could she have been so fooled by a man who was the opposite of everything she'd thought he was? After that experience, she doubted if her battered heart could survive being hurt again.

Then Scott Michaels had walked into the station for his first day of work, and warning signals had clanged in her head. There was something beneath his brooding surface that frightened her, yet intrigued her at the same time. The way his uniform molded to his body and the smile he directed at her reminded her too much of Calvin. When Kate had told her Scott was dealing with some issues in his past, Lisa had made up her mind to keep her distance. Today she knew she was right. The way he'd looked at her made her pulse race—and that could spell disaster.

Letting Scott take her home today wasn't a good idea. She clenched her fists and pounded her knees. There was no way she would ever welcome the friendship of a man who dealt with secrets from the past. She would call Kate and ask her to come pick her up. Then she could apologize to Scott later.

As if she'd willed it, her cell phone ringtone chimed. She set her coffee cup on the table by her bed and pulled the phone from her purse. "Hello."

"Hi, Lisa. It's Kate. You still doing okay?"

Lisa smiled and snuggled down under the covers. "I'm fine. Just waiting for Doc to tell me I can go home."

"Good. I'd offer to come get you, but since I'm filling in for you at dispatch today, I can't leave the station."

Lisa's smile faded. "Oh, yeah. What about Brock, that sweet husband of yours? Can he come get me?"

"I'm afraid not. He has a full day planned. Sheriff Baxter's on the island today, and they're over at the lighthouse right now talking with the park rangers. Betsy's taken Emma to the mainland on a shopping trip. I think they're going to surprise me with some baby clothes. How about Scott? I'm sure he'd be glad to come get you."

"He's already offered."

"Don't you want him to do it?" Kate's voice held a hint of surprise.

Lisa closed her eyes and rubbed her forehead. She couldn't let Kate think she didn't want to be around her brother. "I really don't know Scott well, and I don't want to impose."

Kate's chuckle rang in Lisa's ear. "He wouldn't have offered if he thought you were imposing. He's really a nice guy, Lisa. You need to get to know him better."

"That's what you say to me about every single man on the island. It makes me wonder if you're not trying to help me find a reason for staying here."

"You think so, huh?" Kate paused before she spoke again. "I can't stand to think about you leaving, but I know your mind is made up. So for now, you take care of yourself, and I'll check on you after you get home."

"Thanks, Kate."

After she laid the phone down, Lisa sank back on the pillows and stared up at the ceiling. She was being ridiculous. Scott Michaels wasn't Calvin Jamison, and she wasn't about to fall in love with him. He'd been kind enough to offer to take her home, and she would let him. But after that, she wouldn't encourage any contact with him.

Later that afternoon, Scott followed Lisa from the driveway of her house to the back porch. "I'm still not convinced you should come back home. Are you sure you want to do this?"

Lisa climbed up the two steps to the back porch and stopped at the door. She turned and propped her hands on her hips. "We've already been through this. I'm not going to change my mind."

He shook his head in resignation. "All right. I just hope you know what you're doing."

She pulled her key ring from her purse and smiled at him. "Thanks again for bringing my purse to the hospital. That was very thoughtful of you."

He felt his face grow warm. "It was nothing."

Lisa unlocked the back door of her house and stepped into the kitchen. "Oh, no!"

"What is it?" Scott tried to peer around Lisa, but she blocked his view.

Lisa whirled to face him. Her wide eyes reflected the fear he had seen on her face when she had regained consciousness the day before. "I can't believe this."

Scott pushed past her and entered the kitchen. He stopped in shock at the scene before him. Every drawer in the room had been pulled out, and the contents dumped on the floor. The refrigerator door stood open, and food from inside it had been thrown against the walls. Through the doorway that led to the living room, Scott could see the intruder had not stopped his rampage in the kitchen.

Lisa brushed against him to reenter the room, but he held his hand out to stop her. "Don't go in. Is your cell phone in your purse?"

"Yes."

"Good. Stay on the porch and call the station for backup while I check the house. Whoever did this may still be inside."

"O-okay."

Behind him he heard her making the call for backup. He reached for his gun and winced. Since he was off duty, his gun was at home.

Reason told him he should wait until Brock arrived to help him search the house. If the thief was still inside, though, he could slip out a side window and escape while they were waiting for help. Ignoring the warnings flashing in his mind, Scott eased through the kitchen into the living room.

He stopped in the doorway and stared in shock. The sofa cushions had been sliced open and the stuffing pulled out. Overturned end tables, shattered lamps and torn books lay scattered about the room. But it wasn't the destruction of the furnishings that made the hair on the back of his neck stand up. It was something more sinister.

A message scrawled in red paint seemed to leap from the room's white wall and kick him in the stomach. *"Calvin sends his regards."*

Scott took a step backward and gulped a deep breath. He'd often said nothing surprised him after all the senseless acts he'd seen people do to each other in his work, but this did. The break-ins at Lisa's house had been personal, not the work of a random thief.

At the moment he had no clue who had a vendetta against her, but he was determined to find out.

THREE

Thirty minutes later, they stood on Lisa's back porch with Brock Gentry, the chief deputy on the island. Scott still couldn't believe the condition of the rooms inside. Lisa's theory of a random burglary wasn't being considered anymore.

"It's almost as if somebody has been watching the house. When I came by here last night to put the plywood in the window, everything was all right." The muscle in Scott's jaw twitched. "I wish I had walked in on this guy's fun. He would have wished he'd never set foot in here."

Brock pushed his sunglasses up on his nose and nodded. "Yeah, it took him some time to do all his work. He must have known Lisa wouldn't be home." He glanced her way. "Where did he get that red paint he used to write his message?"

"It was in the kitchen. I bought it for painting the walls in there."

Brock frowned. "And now it's splashed over

nearly every wall in the house. Whoever did this made sure every room was hit."

Fear flickered in Lisa's eyes. "I can't imagine why anybody would hate me enough to do so much damage. Yesterday I thought it was a burglar, but this is much more personal."

Brock nodded. "You're right, and that's what concerns me. This wasn't about stealing something that might bring a few bucks."

Scott turned to Brock. "Can you think of anybody who could be involved?"

"Not at the moment." The chief deputy took a deep breath. "I don't mean to pry into your personal life, Lisa, but Kate has told me about Calvin."

Lisa snorted. "Yeah, I can really pick a great guy, can't I?"

Brock frowned and shook his head. "It's not that. I was wondering if you know any of his friends who still live on the island. We need to look at them as persons of interest first."

Lisa thought for a moment before she replied. "I know Calvin used to hang out some with Skip Matlock, who owns the Blue Pelican Bar and Grill. And there was Andy McKay, who works on the ferry. Those are the only ones who come to mind right now."

Brock pulled a small notepad from his pocket

and wrote the names down. "That's okay. I'll ask Kate if she knows anyone else. I'll check on these guys and see what I can find out."

Scott detected a slight tremor in Lisa's shoulders. She was trying to keep her fear from showing, but it was revealed in the frown that wrinkled her forehead.

She took a deep breath and raised her chin. "It seems obvious someone has a grudge against me. What should I do?"

Brock tilted his head and stared at her. "Why don't you come to our house until we catch this guy? Kate and I would love to have you."

Lisa smiled. "That won't be necessary. I called Treasury Wilkes over at the Island Connection Bed-and-Breakfast and told her what happened. She insisted I stay there as long as I needed. I'll feel safe there."

Scott breathed a sigh of relief. "Good. Since she's a second mother to my sisters, I inherited that privilege, too. She'll take good care of you."

Brock glanced at his watch. "I need to get back on patrol. Scott, can you follow Lisa to Treasury's place?"

"I thought I'd help her clean up some, and then we'll go." He turned to Lisa. "If that's all right with you."

The smile that creased her lips made his pulse

race. "Thank you, Scott. I don't know what I would have done without you during this ordeal."

"Like I said—the Ocracoke deputies aim to please."

Out of the corner of his eye, Scott saw Brock bite his lip, but he couldn't control the grin that spread across his face. He slapped Scott on the back. "Spoken like a dedicated lawman."

Lisa smiled at Brock. "I'm lucky to have such good friends looking out for me." She turned to Scott. "So, are you ready to get to work?"

"Uh, yeah. I'll be there in a minute."

When she entered the house, he faced Brock. "What's so funny that you were about to burst out laughing?"

Brock chuckled and punched him in the arm. "Oh, I suppose it was those big calf eyes of yours that can't get enough of looking at Lisa."

Scott's mouth gaped open. "What are you talking about?"

"Don't act like you don't know what I'm talking about, brother. Kate and I have seen how you look at Lisa at the station. You're interested in her, and we're happy for you. We think it's time you got on with your life."

A weight like a heavy anvil bore down on his chest and almost crushed the breath from him. He let out a long sigh. "You know I can't think about things like that, Brock. I wouldn't wish my problems on any woman."

The smile vanished from Brock's face, and he placed his hand on Scott's shoulder. "In the year since you came to Ocracoke, I've come to like and respect you, Scott. What happened while you were on military missions is in the past. Your doctors say you've made miraculous strides in overcoming your PTSD. All you have to do is believe it, too."

Scott shook his head. "I don't know if I can ever forget what I saw, Brock. It haunts me every day of my life."

"Then we all have to continue to pray. God can bring you through this."

"He's gotten me this far. I want to believe He can make me feel like a whole person again, but it's rough dealing with the past."

"Give it some time." Brock glanced at his watch and sighed. "I've got to go. I'll check with you later to see how things are going here."

"Thanks, Brock. It sure is nice to have a brother-in-law who's also a friend."

Brock clamped his hand on Scott's shoulder and squeezed. "Glad to have you in the family."

Scott stuck his hands in his pockets and stared after Brock's retreating figure. Instead of feeling good about what his brother-in-law had just said, the old anger rose up inside him. How could his aunt have lied to him all those years when he'd asked about his father? Now he would never know the man who had spent his life looking for the son who had been stolen.

He thought of how much Kate, Betsy and Emma had come to mean to him. His anger toward the aunt who'd raised him intensified. What had made her kidnap him? Did she in some way blame his father for his mother's death? These questions had haunted him ever since his sisters had found him, but there would never be answers. His aunt had taken them to the grave with her five years ago.

Because of her, he had missed the joy of seeing three younger sisters grow up. He wondered what it would have been like to see Kate and Betsy go on their first dates or to watch them play sports. Or for Emma to take her first steps. They had told him over and over he had to forgive his aunt for what she had done, but he didn't think that was possible. She had robbed him of the life he should have had.

When he was a child, his questions about his father and other family members had been brushed aside. His aunt's refusal to answer and her stern, unloving manner had made him feel alone, as if no one had ever wanted him. Maybe that was what had driven him to volunteer for every dangerous mission in the army that came along. In the end, he'd paid dearly. It had taken a toll on him and left him so emotionally damaged he didn't think he would ever have a relationship with a woman. Especially not a woman like Lisa Wade.

An hour later, Scott reentered the kitchen and set an empty trash can on the floor. "I dumped that load in your big garbage can and hauled it to the end of the driveway. I'll give the sanitation crew a call in the morning and ask them to make a special trip out here to empty it."

"You don't have to do that," she said. "You've done enough just helping me clean up. I don't want to impose."

"You're not imposing, Lisa. I want to help."

Her lips quivered, and her eyes filled with tears. "I—I just…"

He took a step closer. "Look, Lisa, you don't have to be brave for me. You've had your home invaded twice by someone who seems bent on revenge. That would frighten anyone. So don't think you have to put up a strong front for me."

She wiped at her eyes and took a deep breath. "Thanks, Scott. It's just that all my life it seems I've had to stand on my own two feet."

He nodded. "I know the feeling. I suppose we have a lot in common. But you have friends.

Brock, Kate and I will do everything we can to keep you safe."

She smiled, and her tears glistened. "Thanks, Scott. I suppose I'm more fortunate than a lot of people."

A desire to put his arms around her swept over him, but he jammed his hands in his pockets and cleared his throat. "Now let's see what we need to do next. We've worked on the living room and the kitchen. Where to now?"

She pushed her long hair behind her ear and sighed. "Okay, if you insist. There's a room at the back of the house we haven't used in years. It was my parents' bedroom before their deaths. I looked in there, and my *visitor* tore everything out of the closet we used for storage. I'd like to straighten the room up. Maybe pick out the things I need to throw away."

"Sure. I'll help you."

She hesitated for a moment as if she was debating whether or not to say something. "I do have a job in there that requires someone taller than I am."

"What?"

"It's the closet. One end is filled with shelves that cover the entire width. The other end has a rod for clothes, but it only goes from front to back. I thought I could make room for hanging more clothes if I tore out the shelves and ran a rod the length of the closet." She furrowed her brow. "But I'm not tall enough to reach the top shelves, and I don't like to stand on ladders."

A grin pulled at his mouth. "Don't tell me you're afraid of heights."

He expected her to grin at his words. Instead something akin to sorrow shadowed her face. "I have been ever since I was a child."

Something in her manner told him not to press the subject. "I guess we all have our fears. Let's go take a look at that closet."

Lisa led the way down a hall to a bedroom at the back of the house. When they stepped into the room, Scott shook his head in disgust at the scattered clothes, books and papers that littered the floor. "Your burglar really made a mess in here. Did you say this was your parents' bedroom?"

Lisa nodded as she surveyed the damage. "My parents moved in with my father's mother when they married. My grandmother told me my mother wanted to move out when I was born, but my father refused. He was a fisherman and was gone for days at a time. He felt we were safer living with his mother." She paused for a moment. "After both my parents died, I grew up here with my grandmother. She closed this room off, though, and we never used it except for storage."

"It wouldn't take much to fix this room up. Paint

the walls, get rid of the old carpet, and it could add to the value of your house."

"I thought so, too. Let me show you the closet." They stepped over a pile of books, and she opened the closet door and pointed to the shelves at one end of the closet. "They're right there. I hope they won't be too hard to get out."

He stepped into the closet, took hold of the bottom shelf, and pulled. "Piece of cake. A little paint and a new rod in here, and you'll have a bigger and better closet."

"Are you sure you don't mind taking the shelves out?"

"Not a bit. By the way, you know last night was my last rotation on second shift. I go back on days tomorrow. I'd be glad to come back tomorrow night and help you some more."

She hesitated for a moment. "Th-that's nice of you, Scott, but I wouldn't feel right asking you to do it again."

A warning flashed in his mind. He had already gotten closer to Lisa than he'd intended. Continuing to be around her could put him at serious risk of becoming too involved, and that would be bad for both of them.

He gave a slight shake of his head. What was he thinking? After all, he was a deputy, and Lisa was the victim of a crime. She needed protection until they caught her intruder. He inhaled deeply. "You're not asking—I'm volunteering. It's not safe for you to be here alone until we know who broke into your house. I'll pick you up at Treasury's after supper."

He expected her to protest again. Instead her mouth curled into a smile. "Thank you, Scott. I'm going back to work tomorrow. Since you'll be on the day shift, how about if I buy you dinner at the Brass Lantern after we get off work? It's the least I can do to repay you for all you've done for me."

A thrill shot through him at her words, but he tried to ignore it. The smart thing would be for him to tell Lisa he couldn't go to dinner. He opened his mouth to refuse her kind offer, but the sparkle in her blue eyes weakened his defenses.

So instead he heard himself speaking words that left him wondering what hold this woman was beginning to have on him. "I'd like to go to dinner with you," he said.

Lisa's heart felt lighter than it had since she'd come home to the sound of a burglar in her house. She didn't know what had lifted her mood, but she suspected it might have something to do with the handsome police officer who hummed a tune as he pulled another shelf from the closet wall.

"What's that song?"

Scott handed her the shelf and grinned. "Something we sang at church last Sunday."

"Oh, so you go to church with your sisters?"

He wiped the perspiration from his forehead and nodded. "Yeah. Kate said she's tried to get you to go, but she hasn't convinced you yet."

"No."

"We'd all like for you to come."

Her skin warmed, and suddenly the room felt stuffy. She turned away and laid the shelf on top of the other two he'd already dismantled. "I don't think the air conditioner is working. I wonder if I need to get a repairman out here to check the ductwork."

She glanced back at Scott, but he seemed focused on the next shelf. He shrugged. "Maybe so."

At the thought she groaned. The changes she was making had already exceeded the budget she'd set. Now with all the additional damage, she doubted her insurance would cover the costs. If it didn't, where would she get the extra money? The house wouldn't sell unless it was in good condition. And if the house didn't sell, she couldn't leave the island. She had no idea what she would do then.

A tremor went through her body. Did someone really hate her enough to do all this damage? And what if her attacker had decided to bludgeon her to death while she was unconscious? The questions made chills run up and down her spine. She struggled to direct her thoughts to something more positive.

With an effort she turned her attention to Scott

and peered into the closet. "How are you making out in there?"

"It's a little warm, but I'm on the last shelf. I'll… uh-oh, I didn't see that coming." He ducked and covered his head as the closet's top shelf toppled downward and clattered to the floor at his feet.

Lisa crowded into the closet to get a better look. "What happened?"

Scott straightened and pointed to a spot high up on the closet wall. "There are two wood brackets attached to the wall, and the shelf was resting on top of them. It fell when I pulled on it."

Lisa stared upward at the brackets sticking out from the wall. "I've never noticed those being there, but I hardly ever came in here. When I did, I would put something in the closet floor or on one of the bottom shelves. I couldn't reach the top one."

Scott shook his head. "Neither could anyone else unless they stood on a chair." He flashed a smile in her direction. "Which explains why you never noticed them."

Lisa's eyebrows arched, and she narrowed her eyes. "I should never have told you about my fear of heights." Placing her hands on her hips, she studied the top of the closet. "I wonder why they made it that way."

"I don't know. Do you have anything I can stand on to get those brackets off the wall?"

"Yes. I have a two-step folding kitchen ladder,

unless it got broken today. Let me find it." Minutes later, she returned from the kitchen with the ladder in hand. "Here it is. He must not have seen it in the utility room."

Scott unfolded it and climbed onto the higher step. Lisa stuck her head around the corner of the door and watched as Scott reached up and grasped one of the brackets.

"Whoa, now. What is this?" he asked.

Lisa stood on her tiptoes and tried to get a better look. "What's the matter?"

Without answering, he wrapped his fingers around both brackets and pulled. The board they were nailed to slipped free of the wall. "I don't believe this."

Lisa's stomach fluttered. "What did you find?"

"What I thought was the closet wall isn't at all. The real wall is behind it."

"Are you saying somebody built a false wall at the end of the closet? Why would anybody do that?"

"I don't know." He handed the board that had covered the opening down to Lisa. "It could have been done when the house was built. Maybe the owner wanted a place to hide valuables." He stuck his hand in the hole and reached downward.

Lisa dropped the board at her feet and directed her attention back to him. "Be careful, Scott. There may be spiders in there."

A laugh rumbled in his throat. "Spiders? That's just like a woman. Find a secret hiding place, and she's worried about spiders inside." Surprise flashed across his face. "Well, what do we have here?"

"What is it?"

"There's a metal box wedged down in here. I'm going to pry it free. It looks like it's been here a long time."

"Can you get it?"

"I just about have..." He grunted and gave a tug. "I have it." He hopped to the floor of the closet and held out the metal box to her. "Here it is."

Lisa grabbed a cloth that stuck out of one of the storage boxes and wiped the dust from the container. There was no lock. "This is like something you'd see on TV. I feel like I've stepped back in time and am about to find something that belonged to one of my ancestors."

He grinned. "Or it could be an empty box that fell down in there years ago."

Lisa raised her eyebrows. "I like my version better. In fact, I predict it contains jewels hidden in the wall to keep thieves from finding them."

Scott laughed and shook his head. "Dream on. But what are you waiting for? Open it and find out what's in it."

They dropped down on the floor side by side. Lisa placed the box in her lap and put her hand on its top. Before she could open it, Scott placed his hand on top of hers. "Seriously, though, you do realize this may be nothing, right?"

"Of course. I just thought the moment called for a little drama."

He smiled. "I just don't want you to be too disappointed if there's nothing inside."

"I won't." Even as she said it, she knew it wasn't true. Her grandmother had told her the house was built by Lisa's great-grandfather. Whatever lay inside the walls had to belong to one of her family members.

Biting down on her lip, Lisa pulled the top up and stared down at the contents of the box. "There's a small black book inside." She reached inside, pulled it out and held it up.

"What kind of book is it?" Scott asked.

"I don't know." She opened the cover, gasped and jumped to her feet. The book along with the box fell to the floor. Lisa jammed her fist in her mouth to stifle the moan that rose in her throat.

Scott sprang up from the floor, his eyes wide. He grabbed her by the arms and turned her to face him. "Lisa, what's the matter?"

Her heart pounded so hard she could hardly speak. "I can't believe it, Scott. This may answer all my questions."

He frowned and shook his head. "I don't understand."

She wriggled free of his hold, scooped up the

book and clutched it to her chest. She sank back onto the floor. "The first page of this book is inscribed with my mother's name. It says it's her journal."

"You're kidding." He eased down next to her. "I can understand why you would be happy about finding something that belonged to your mother. But you're acting like this is something more than just a diary."

"It is. You see, I don't remember my parents. My father and mother both died when I was three. He was lost at sea during a storm, and she died a few weeks later. I've never really known anything about either of them." She caressed the book in her hand. "Maybe now I can come to know my mother."

Sympathy filled his eyes. "I know what it's like to want to know more about a parent who's died. I hope your mother's journal will help you."

Her heart skipped a beat because she realized Scott had no idea why she would be so interested in the diary. "Has Kate ever told you about my mother?"

He shook his head. "No. She just told me you were orphaned when you were three. Why would she tell me anything else?"

"Because everybody on the island knows the story, and I thought you might have heard it by now." She held up the book. "Maybe my mother's journal will finally give me the answers I've always wanted."

"Story? Answers? What are you talking about?"

Lisa took a deep breath. "I want to know why my mother left me alone with my grandmother one night when I was three years old, climbed to the top of the island lighthouse and jumped to her death from the widow's walk."

Scott's face looked as if she had thrown ice water on him. "Your mother committed suicide by jumping from the lighthouse?"

"Yes, just a few weeks after my father's death."

Understanding flashed across his face. "Is that what triggered your fear of heights?"

She bit her lip and nodded. "Yes. When I was growing up, the park rangers would take kids up to the widow's walk sometimes. I never could do it, though. My friends would tell me how you could see the whole island from up there, but I could never go. I get sick to my stomach just thinking about climbing up there."

"It must be rough seeing the oldest lighthouse in North Carolina every day."

"It is. Since it's still in operation, I can't even escape it at night. Whenever I go out, I see its light. So I'm reminded of my mother's death day and night."

"And you never went up to the widow's walk?"

"No. In fact, I go out of my way so that I don't

have to drive by the lighthouse. I don't even want to see the entrance."

He straightened and glanced at the book she held. "Are you sure you want to read what she wrote? It may hurt too much to read about her grief over your father's death."

She shook her head. "She wasn't grieving, according to my grandmother. She told me often enough she was the only one who cared when he died. I could tell that she never liked my mother, but I wondered if she was right. Now I can find out."

"And what good will that do? You can't change the past, just like I can't change the fact my aunt withheld the truth from me for years."

"I know, but it's different with you, Scott. You have your sisters now, and I'll never have anyone. All my family is dead, and I have to know why."

He studied her for a moment before he nodded. "All right. But understand that you may not like what you find."

She took a deep breath and picked up the book again. Holding it, she flipped through page after page of neat handwriting. When she came to the last page, her gaze roved over the lines until she came to the last one. She read it, frowned and read it again.

"I don't understand this."

Scott leaned closer. "What?"

"This last entry was written the day she died. That date has been burned in my mind all my life. But listen to the last thing she wrote. *I don't regret anything I have done. It's all been for my sweet Lisa. Someday she will be a very rich woman.*"

"Rich? What do you think she meant? Could she have left some money for you somewhere?"

Lisa closed the book, laid it in her lap and pressed her palms on the cover. "I don't know, but I intend to find out. And this book is going to help me do it."

A small beam of hope ignited in her heart. Just a few minutes ago, she had been agonizing over who could have done so much damage to her home and made her feel as though she was in danger. Now, thanks to Scott, she had discovered something that might answer all her questions surrounding her mother's sudden death.

In the span of twenty-four hours, she'd experienced numerous emotions—fear for her life, anxiety over the destruction of her belongings, hopelessness at how much the vandalism was going to cost her and uncertainty about her future. She clasped the journal to her chest and smiled. None of those mattered if she could finally put to rest the one emotion that had haunted her all her life—rejection.

For as long as she could remember, she had felt her mother would never have killed herself if she had loved her daughter. Maybe the journal would finally give her an answer. If it did, she knew she could face anything—and anyone—who tried to harm her.

FOUR

Lisa gripped the journal tighter in her hands as she reentered the living room. As long as she could remember, she'd wondered about her mother and wished for a memory of the beautiful woman in the small, dog-eared photo she kept in her wallet. Now her mother's words had found their way across the lonely years to the daughter who had hungered for her love.

At last she might be able to discover things about her mother other women's daughters took for granted. What was her favorite color? Did she like music? As a girl, what had she wanted to be when she grew up? But there was one burning question Lisa wanted answered more than anything else. Did Roxanne Wade love the daughter she left behind when she'd jumped from the widow's walk of the lighthouse?

A discreet cough from behind reminded her she wasn't alone. The sound sent a tingle of awareness through her. Since Scott had come to work for the sheriff's department, she had never thought of him as anything other than a coworker. The time she'd spent with him in the last twenty-four hours had changed all that, and she was glad he was the one who had found her mother's diary.

"Are you all right, Lisa?"

She smiled and turned toward him. "I am. I'm happier than I've been in a long time."

A flicker of concern crossed his face. "Let me remind you…"

She held up a hand to stop him. "I know what you're going to say. I'm not expecting all my questions to be answered. For now, just having my mother's words with me is all I care about. At least I have a part of her." She closed her eyes for a moment and frowned. "Sometimes I lie awake at night and try to remember what her voice sounded like or what her perfume smelled like, but nothing comes to mind. At least I'll be able to know what she thought about. Maybe even find out what led her to kill herself."

"I just don't want you to be hurt."

She smiled and squeezed his arm. "Don't worry about me, Scott. There's an empty spot in my heart reserved for my mother. Maybe I can fill it with something from this diary."

He glanced down at her hand on his arm. "I hope so."

Before she could respond, a knock at the door

caught her attention. Fear rippled through her body, and she frowned. Her intruder probably had hoped his visits would have a lingering effect on her, but she couldn't allow him to have that control over her. It was ridiculous to be afraid of someone knocking at the door.

She squared her shoulders and glanced at Scott. "Who could that be?"

She started toward the door, but Scott stepped around her. "Let me answer it. You stay behind me."

Lisa followed close behind him to the front door. He glanced over his shoulder and frowned. "Were you expecting anybody?"

"No. It might be Jeff stopping by to check on me."

Scott took a deep breath and eased the door open. His shoulders relaxed as he exhaled. "Grady Teach, what are you doing here?"

"I heard Lisa done had another break-in, and I came by to see if'n she was all right." Grady's shrill voice pierced Lisa's ears.

She peeked around Scott and smiled. "Grady, come on in."

They stepped back for him to enter, and Grady strutted into the house. Lisa cast a quick glance in Scott's direction and tried to keep from smiling. Grady, who had long been recognized as the unofficial island historian, made it his business to keep up with everything that happened to the residents of his island. As a descendant of Edward Teach, better known as Blackbeard, the pirate who had made Ocracoke Island his home, Grady felt his family's long history with this tiny speck of land off the coast of North Carolina had given him the authority to oversee all the happenings on this island. Most residents, however, regarded him as the biggest gossip in the village.

Shaking his head, Grady stopped in the middle of the living room, planted his legs in a wide stance and pulled his straw hat off the long, gray hair that hung over his ears. "Looks like somebody's done taken a dislike to you, Lisa. Got any ideas who it could be?"

"No."

He glanced around the room, and he glared at the message scrawled in red paint on the living room wall. "Calvin, huh? You think he done hired somebody to scare you?"

"I don't know. It's a possibility."

Grady nodded. "I was over to the Blue Pelican, and I happened to overhear Brock talking to Skip Matlock. Seems like Brock might be thinkin' that Calvin could have asked Skip to do some dirty work for him."

Scott cast a quick glance at Lisa. "What did Skip say, Grady?"

"Oh, nothing much. Seems like he's been off the

island for the past week. Came in on the last ferry this afternoon and went straight to work. Hasn't been out of the building since."

The fear Lisa had tried to force from her mind returned with a vengeance. Her legs trembled, and she sank down on the sofa that Scott had set upright. The stuffing from the pillows still protruded through the slashes made by the intruder.

"So, it wasn't Skip who broke in here. Why didn't Brock call and let me know?"

Scott dropped down beside her. "Skip was only one person of interest. There are others. Brock is busy doing his job, and he'll let you know when he has any information." He gave her hand a reassuring squeeze. "And I'll be helping him tomorrow. We're going to find who did this."

Grady inched closer and cocked his head to one side. "So you fellers think somebody else might be the bad guy here? Who would that be?"

Scott's lips thinned into a straight line. "I can't say at this point, Grady. Everybody could be a suspect right now." He stood and arched an eyebrow. "So where were you this afternoon, Grady?"

Surprise flashed across Grady's face, and he took a step backward. "I was doin' what I do every day. I was out in the salt marshes lookin' for Blackbeard's treasure."

Scott glanced at Lisa, and she detected the slight

grin pulling at his mouth. He advanced on Grady. "Are you sure?"

Lisa jumped up and laid a restraining hand on Scott's arm. "I think you're scaring Grady. I'm sure he's telling the truth."

Grady straightened to his full height and glared at Scott. "I reckon I am. Everybody on the island could tell you that. But you being such a newcomer, I expect you don't know me yet. Just ask your sister Kate. She'll tell you I'm an honest feller, and I wouldn't hurt nobody on my island."

Scott nodded. "I've heard that. It's just that a law officer can't overlook anybody." He turned to Lisa and winked. "So I guess I'll take your word for it that you were looking for treasure this afternoon."

Grady gave a snort of disgust. "Nice to see you believe me. Now I guess I better get on home." He glanced at the journal in Lisa's hand. "What's that you got there?"

She held the book up. "We found this in a closet in the back of the house. It's my mother's journal."

Grady's eyes lit up with interest. "You don't say." He rubbed his chin and stared at the book for a moment. "Roxanne was a real nice lady. Prettiest girl I'd ever seen when your daddy brought her back from the mainland as his wife."

Lisa's heart pumped, and she clutched the journal against her chest. "You never told me you knew my mother."

He frowned. "Well, your grandmother didn't want nobody to talk to you about her. She said no woman who left her daughter like she did deserved to even be mentioned." Grady shook his head. "Sometimes your grandmother could be a hard woman to deal with."

"I know. She never would talk to me about my mother." Lisa looked at the book. "Maybe now I can find out what made her commit suicide."

Grady nodded. "I hope so." His forehead wrinkled into a frown when he glanced at Scott. "Well, I'd better be goin' before I get accused of some other crime on the island. I'll be checking on you, Lisa, to make sure you're okay."

"Thanks, Grady."

When Lisa had closed the door behind Grady, she turned to Scott and laughed. "I've never seen Grady so flustered. You really scared him."

A grin spread across Scott's face. "I couldn't resist. Ever since I've been here, I've heard how Grady is the island authority on everything that's happening. Kate once said his news gets to the island grapevine quicker than sending a text message."

Lisa shook her head. "I think she's right." She glanced around the house and sighed. "I think we've done enough tonight. We both have to work tomorrow, so we need to get some rest. If you'll give me a few minutes, I'll pack some things to take to Treasury's, and then we'll leave."

"All right. In the meantime, I'll see if there's anything else I can do in your parents' old room."

They walked back down the narrow hallway to the bedrooms. As Lisa turned toward her room, she brushed against Scott, and a small tingle raced up her arm. She glanced up at him, but his cool stare gave no indication he had noticed the brief contact. He turned toward her parents' room, and she entered hers.

She closed her eyes and rubbed her forehead. What was the matter with her? She'd promised herself she would never become attracted to another man. Even though Scott had been a huge help to her during her ordeal, she couldn't forget the fact that he struggled with a past that still haunted him. She didn't know what had happened to him, but from what Kate had told her, it had left deep scars in his soul. She had enough of her own problems to even think about a man who shouldered a lot of baggage from his past.

Her suitcase lay on the floor where the burglar had pulled it from the closet. She set it on the bed and began to pick up her scattered clothes and put them inside. When she had packed enough for a few days, she laid the journal on top.

A thump from her parents' room reminded her that Scott was still working. Since their first meeting, she had thought him reserved and serious. Tonight a different side of his personality had surfaced when he'd teased Grady, and she liked the part of him he seemed to guard with such care. And his deep-set blue eyes. Sometimes they took her breath away when they stared straight into her soul.

No. I will not do this.

She glanced down at the journal she'd placed in the suitcase. All she wanted was to find out more about her mother. Maybe then she'd be free of her past and could leave the island to begin a new life somewhere else.

The next morning Scott, juggling a cardboard carton that held two cups of coffee and a small white sack, closed the door of The Coffee Cup and stepped onto the sidewalk in front of the shop. A group of teenagers on bicycles waved to him from the street. He gave a nod and smiled. Off to the beach, no doubt.

He'd traveled the world, but he'd never seen beaches like the ones at Ocracoke. How he wished he had grown up here. His life would have been so different if he'd lived with his father and his second family. He shook his head to rid it of thoughts of things that could never be and headed toward his police cruiser parked at the curb.

"Scott, wait up a minute."

The familiar voice brought a smile to his face. He turned to see his three sisters hurrying toward him. Emma, who'd recently had her eleventh birthday, ran ahead of Kate and Betsy.

Emma came to a stop next to him and grinned up at him. He reached out with his free hand and cupped her chin. "Hi, princess. I didn't expect to see you today."

She pointed to their sisters. "We're on our way to the Island General Store. We're going to bake a cake for Treasury's birthday. You're going to be home for dinner Friday night, aren't you?"

"You bet I am. I wouldn't miss Treasury's birthday."

"Good." She glanced at the sack. "What's that?"

"Blueberry muffins. Why? Are you hungry?"

She grinned. "I sure would like to have a donut."

He laughed and pulled a five-dollar bill from his pocket. "Get a donut and something to drink."

She grabbed the money and gave him a quick hug. "Thanks, Scott. You're the best brother any girl could have."

Kate and Betsy came to a stop beside him and stared after their little sister. Kate shook her head. Her chestnut-colored hair brushed her shoulders, and she arched an eyebrow. "You're spoiling her, Scott."

"I thought that's what big brothers were supposed to do." The door to The Coffee Cup slammed behind Emma, but he continued to stare after her. A lump formed in his throat at how much she had come to mean to him. "And I've got a lot of years to catch up on."

The two sisters glanced at each other before Betsy smiled, the dimples in her cheeks deepening. She reached out and grasped his arm. "You're here now, and that's the most important thing."

Moisture threatened to flood his eyes. He blinked and looked around in hopes that no one had witnessed the momentary lapse in his demeanor. It wouldn't do to have Grady Teach telling everybody that the new deputy had weeped right on the village's main street. He drew in a long breath. "You're right, and I don't want to waste a minute of our time together."

A mischievous smile pulled at Betsy's mouth. "You know how much Emma and I enjoy having you live at our house since Kate and Brock got a place of their own. It makes dinnertime so special to have you there at night." She inched closer. "So, what time will you be home tonight?"

His face grew warm, and he swallowed. "I—I d-don't know…" Then he caught the teasing look on both his sisters' faces and scowled. "Quit it, you two. I can tell you know I'm going to have dinner with Lisa tonight."

They burst out laughing, and Kate nodded. "I called the police station this morning and asked her to come over for dinner tonight. She told me the two of you are going out."

"It's not what you think. She only wants to thank me for helping her after her break-ins."

Betsy rolled her eyes at Kate. "Sure she does. And I'm sure you're willing to be thanked."

Scott cocked an eyebrow. "Betsy, cut it out."

Kate elbowed her sister in the ribs. "Leave him alone, Betsy. We've tried to fix him up with Lisa ever since he got here, so let's not jinx it by teasing him."

He flashed a grateful smile to Kate. "Thanks, sis."

Kate's face grew serious, and she took a step closer to him. "Seriously, though, Brock and I are worried about those burglaries at Lisa's house. Maybe it's because I know what it's like to be targeted by a crazed killer, and I'm afraid for her."

His heart thudded at the reminder of the brush with death his three sisters had experienced before he came to Ocracoke. "I don't think her situation is the same as yours was, Kate, but I'm going to keep an eye on her."

She smiled. "Good. Lisa is one of my best friends, and I don't want to see anything happen to her."

"Neither do I." He reached over and kissed both his sisters on the cheek.

Kate tilted her head and pointed her finger at

Scott. "And make sure you don't do anything to hurt her either."

His sister's words stunned Scott, and his eyes narrowed. "You know I'm not interested in getting involved with a woman. Especially not one who happens to be best friends with my sisters."

The door of The Coffee Cup opened, and a man stepped onto the sidewalk. Scott moved toward the curb to let him pass, but the man stopped and faced Kate. "Well, if it isn't former Deputy Kate Michaels—or should I say Kate Gentry, now that you're married." His gaze raked her body. "I heard you were expecting a baby."

"Ean Thornton," she said. "I haven't seen you around much lately."

Hatred glared from his eyes. "I spend a lot of my time at the state prison visiting my son. You remember him, don't you? After all, you're the one who picked on him all the time he was growing up."

Kate shook her head. "I'm sorry about your son, Ean, but he made some bad decisions. Especially when he decided to commit murder."

He shook his finger at her. "It's all your fault he's in prison, and someday you're going to pay for it."

Scott stepped in front of Ean. "Don't threaten my sister, Thornton. From what I heard your son got exactly what was coming to him."

His eyebrows arched, and he gave a sarcastic chuckle. "You're new to our island and don't know what's gone on here for years. A lot of people around here have something coming to them. Just make sure you don't get caught in the middle."

He whirled and stormed down the street. When he'd disappeared around the corner, Scott turned back to Kate. "Are you all right?"

She sighed. "Yeah. When I was chief deputy, Ean accused me of persecuting his son Mike every time I stopped him for speeding or driving under the influence. He now blames me because Mike's in prison for murder." She rubbed her stomach. "I hope this little one doesn't put me through what Mike has done to his parents."

Scott laughed. "Not a chance. You and Betsy have been great mothers to Emma, and you're going to be terrific with this baby." He glanced down at the sack he held. "My coffee's getting cold. I need to get going. Tell Emma I'll catch up with her later."

They waved to him as he climbed into his police cruiser and pulled into traffic. Try as he might, he couldn't put his conversation with his sisters out of his mind. They acted as if he and Lisa were already involved. If that's what they thought, he'd have to make sure they understood his interest in Lisa was strictly professional.

All he wanted was to find out who had attacked Lisa and trashed her house. From what he'd been able to ascertain, Lisa had no enemies. In fact, she was well liked by everyone who knew her. A chill ran through his body. A year ago, Kate had thought only Ean and Mike Thornton hated her, but she'd been wrong. She experienced the worst time of her life when a seemingly meek person who was in reality a sadistic killer had arrived on Ocracoke and targeted her. Could something like that be behind the attempts to frighten Lisa? Or was it that, as they suspected, Calvin Jamison wanted to get back at her for the imagined wrongs she had done him.

He tightened his hand on the steering wheel and gritted his teeth. Whoever was behind the burglaries at Lisa's house had to be stopped—and soon—before someone ended up getting hurt. He didn't want that someone to be Lisa.

Lisa had tried all morning to concentrate on her job, but her thoughts kept straying to the journal she'd tucked inside her desk drawer when she'd come to work. Although she'd wanted to open it last night when she got back to Treasury's bed-and-breakfast, she couldn't bring herself to do it. She had no idea why her hand froze each time she started to turn to the first page. Maybe she was scared of what she would find, then perhaps the fear that her mother had never really loved her would be proven true in the written words.

With a sigh she tried once again to pull her

thoughts away from the book. The front door to the police station opened, and Scott Michaels walked into the room. His hair appeared damp with perspiration, but his blue eyes held a gleam of surprise.

He held a small cardboard carton containing a white bag and two cups of coffee. Lisa's heart shriveled at The Coffee Cup's logo on the sack. Scott smiled and set the container on her desk. "I bought some coffee and blueberry muffins. I thought we could treat ourselves to something for a break."

Lisa blinked at the tears in the corners of her eyes. How many times had Calvin brought her something from The Coffee Cup? At the time she'd thought it was because he was interested in her, but she had been proven wrong.

She tried to speak, but her vocal cords wouldn't cooperate. Instead she reached for a cup, took a sip and savored the hot liquid that melted the icy feeling in her throat. "Thanks, Scott. That was very nice of you."

He smiled, and she noticed how his mouth crooked up on one side. "I saw my sisters when I was coming out of The Coffee Cup."

She tilted her head to one side. "You did? I talked to Kate this morning."

He chuckled. "Yeah, that's what they said." He took a bite of muffin and pulled a napkin from the sack. "They were going to the store to get groceries for Treasury's birthday celebration on Friday night. Since I'm on days now, I can be home that night. Treasury has come to mean a lot to me, and I don't want to miss her birthday."

"Betsy invited me, too."

"Good." He drained his coffee and tossed the cup in the trash can. "I need to get back on patrol. I'll check in with you from time to time and let you know what's happening around town. I hope we have a quiet afternoon."

"Me, too. And don't forget I'm taking you to dinner."

His gaze swept over her, and the intensity made her tremble. "I haven't forgotten. I'll see you later."

Lisa sat unmoving until the door closed behind him, then she released her pent-up breath. What was the matter with her? Ever since she'd regained consciousness in her living room and seen Scott Michaels bending over her, she hadn't been able to get him out of her mind.

She clenched her fists, pushed back from her desk and stood. She had begun to experience unwelcome feelings where Scott was concerned, and it frightened her. Dinner tonight was supposed to be repayment for his kindness to her. That was supposed to be their one and only social meeting, but she should have known he wouldn't miss Treasury's birthday.

If he was going to be at Kate's on Friday night,

it might be better if she didn't go. She'd no sooner had the thought than she realized how ridiculous she was being. Treasury had taken her in when her house had been vandalized, and it would be rude for her to stay away from the party.

She took a deep breath. Dinner tonight with Scott, then Treasury's party on Friday. After that she would keep her distance from the man who stirred her in ways no one else ever had. Satisfied she had come to the right decision, she sank back into her chair, directed her attention to the computer screen in front of her and tried to ignore the thought that crept into her mind. She might have made the right decision, but she didn't know if she had the willpower to follow through with it.

FIVE

Three p.m. Lisa sighed and rubbed the bump on her head that throbbed. This had been the longest day she'd ever had at work. Maybe she should have taken another day off to recuperate. Luckily for her, the office had been quiet with few calls coming into the station. Of course, only the local residents called the line connected to their office. Tourists with emergencies called 911, and those calls went to the terminal on the mainland, where they were relayed here to Ocracoke. With their island twenty-five miles from the mainland and two and a half hours away by ferry, the county's emergency offices stationed here responded as soon as she received the message.

However, today hadn't seen any emergencies, and she was glad. All she wanted to do was get rid of this headache and tackle the journal in her desk drawer. She still hadn't been able to pull it out even though she wanted to.

Now caught up on all her work, she had an opportunity to peek at the first few pages. She pulled the journal from the drawer, rubbed her fingers over the leather cover and opened it to the first page. Her mother's name written in the middle of the page had the same effect on her as it had the night before. Her breath caught in her throat and her chest squeezed.

Even though tears formed in her eyes, she forced herself to turn the page. She blinked and struggled to make out the neatly written words that flowed in a straight line across the paper.

April 1, 1982.
Has it only been six months since I came to this forsaken island? It seems longer. My life here is very lonely since John is gone to sea for long periods of time, and I haven't made any friends. I have to talk to someone, so I've decided to put my thoughts down in this book. Thank goodness I have a hiding place that no one will suspect. I would never have found it if I had not been trying to store some books on the closet's top shelf. It will be safe from the prying eyes of my mother-in-law, who dislikes me so much. I wish John hadn't insisted we live with his mother. Now I know how a prisoner feels when she wants to break out

of prison. The urge to escape increases every day. I may do that one night soon—wait for her to go to sleep and sneak out for a bit of fun at the Sailors' Catch Pub. It's either do that or die of loneliness.

The tears Lisa had blinked away earlier returned. Her mother's image from the worn photograph she carried returned to her mind, and her heart constricted at the sadness of the words she'd read. When her mother had written those words, she was younger than Lisa was now. In those days, there were even fewer residents on the island, and the tourists hadn't yet discovered this paradise in the Atlantic. It must have seemed a desolate place for a young woman whose husband was a commercial fisherman and was away for extended periods of time. Even if these hadn't been her mother's words, Lisa would have been saddened to think of any young wife with such an unhappy day-to-day life.

"Hey, Lisa. How are you doing after all your excitement?"

Lisa jumped at the unexpected interruption and looked up to see Terry Davidson enter the office. She'd been focused so intently on the journal she hadn't heard the front door open. Glancing down at the journal still open on her desk, she closed it and stuck it back in the drawer. With a shaky smile she folded her hands on her desk and assumed her most professional pose. "Hi, Terry. I'm fine. What brings you here? I hope you don't need assistance from one of our deputies."

He pushed his sunglasses up into the sandy shock of hair that always looked windblown and shook his head. "No, I was at The Coffee Cup this morning, and I heard Grady talking about the break-ins at your house. I thought I'd check on an old friend, especially since I haven't seen you around lately."

She narrowed her eyes and gazed at Terry. They had been classmates at the island school, but they had never been close friends. Why did he feel it necessary to stop by? "It's nice that you thought about me, but everything's okay. It was quite a shock to come home to such a mess, but I'll get it all repaired."

"Any leads on who might have done it?"

"No, not yet, but our deputies are working on it."

He nodded. "Good. Grady said something about you finding your mother's diary. How did that happen?"

Her face grew warm, and she clasped her hands tighter. "We found it while we were cleaning up."

"Wow, that must have been a surprise. All these years after your mother's death, you've found her diary. Of course, I was too young to know her, but I've heard my folks talk about her through the years. I expect they're not the only O'cockers who still wonder why she took her own life that way. Word is that a lot of folks thought she was grieving over your father's death. Do you think that's why she jumped from the lighthouse?"

Lisa took a deep breath. "I don't know."

"Maybe her diary will shed some light on her suicide."

Lisa fidgeted in her chair. She should never have told Grady what they'd found. Now everybody on the island would know. She pushed to her feet and stepped out from behind her desk. "If it does, then I guess I'll have my burglar to thank. But I suppose time will tell."

"I never thought of it that way, but you're right." Terry smiled. "When Grady was telling a bunch of us over at The Coffee Cup about you finding the diary, some of the fellows in there who knew your parents said your mother was a beautiful woman. They mentioned that she used to hang out a lot at the Sailors' Catch while your dad was gone. They said there were a lot of men who wished they'd met her before your dad did."

Lisa's hackles went up. "I don't know anything about that. I was only three when she died."

Terry nodded. "I know. I guess she was lucky

to have your grandmother at home to take care of you at night while she went out."

"Look, Terry, I need to get back to work." She wanted him out before she said something she'd regret.

"Okay. Like I said, I just wanted to check on you. Having your house ransacked and finding your mother's journal all at the same time must have been a shock. Grady said there was a message scrawled on your living room wall." He pursed his lips as if deep in thought. "Umm, something like… 'Calvin sends his regards.' After his arrest last year, do you think he might hold a grudge?"

"I have no idea. Calvin is in prison."

"But he still has friends on Ocracoke. Do you think one of them could be trying to frighten you?"

"Possibly."

A small smile curled his lips, and he studied her for a moment. "What a few days you've had. Your house is broken into twice, a message from a guy you helped send to prison is scrawled on your wall and you find a diary that may answer your questions about your mother's suicide. How are you holding up with all that's happened to you?"

"I'm fine." Her stomach roiled. If Terry didn't get out of here, she was going to scream. She glanced over her shoulder toward the back room of the office. "I hate to rush you off, but I really need to get back to work. There are some files in the other room I need to check, but I appreciate your stopping by. It was good to see you."

He nodded. "Just wanted to make sure you're okay. And good luck with your mother's diary. I hope you get the answers you're looking for."

"Me, too."

She breathed a sigh of relief when Terry disappeared through the door. For some reason, his visit worried her. He had seemed concerned for her, but his questions had almost felt like an interrogation. Something just didn't seem right about his visit.

She sank into the chair behind her desk and stared at the door. After a moment, she sighed and pulled the journal out again. As she read through the next few pages, her mother's unhappiness became even more apparent. The pages were filled with descriptions of her lonely days, tirades by her domineering mother-in-law, arguments with her husband, who seemed to stay away for longer periods of time, and her desperation to escape the life she was living on Ocracoke.

Lisa's heart constricted with each page she read. With a groan she slammed the book closed and stuck it into the oversize purse she always carried. If the diary was going to cause her heartbreak, maybe she shouldn't read it. Scott's warnings about not liking what she would find could very well prove to be true.

She wiped at her eyes and gritted her teeth. At

the moment, her emotions wouldn't allow her to read more, but that would change. It might break her heart to read her mother's unhappy words, but that didn't matter. She had to know what had driven her mother to her death.

Scott had heard Brock and Kate talk about the Brass Lantern, but he'd never been here before. Across the table, Lisa spooned the last bite of strawberry shortcake in her mouth and closed her eyes.

"Umm, that was good."

Scott pushed his plate aside and chuckled. "I'm glad you suggested this place. It's a step up from the Sandwich Shop, where I usually grab a bite when I'm on duty."

He let his gaze drift over the interior of the restaurant. Brass lanterns gave off a soft light from where they hung on wall sconces around the room. Smaller replicas adorned each white-draped table. Soft music drifted on the quiet air and added the right touch for the elegant establishment. The Brass Lantern wasn't a place where tourists brought their children after a day at the beach. Rather it catered to couples who wanted to spend time together in a relaxed atmosphere.

Scott's gaze drifted to the couples seated across the room and came to rest on a man he'd seen earlier today. Ean Thornton, calmer than he'd been when Scott had encountered him before, appeared focused on the woman who sat across from him. As she talked, Ean laughed and pulled a cell phone from his coat pocket. He glanced at the keypad and laid the phone next to his plate.

"Scott, did you hear what I said?"

Surprised, he pulled his attention back to Lisa. "I'm sorry. Did you say something?"

"I asked if you wanted more coffee, but you seemed lost in thought."

He smiled. "I'm sorry if I was ignoring you. I'll try not to be such a wet blanket."

She laughed. "I didn't say you were a wet blanket. Although I probably have been for the past few days."

"You're not, but I wouldn't blame you if you were. With your break-ins and the condition of your house—not to mention finding your mother's diary—I'd say you have the perfect excuse to be distracted."

She picked up her fork and traced the design on the edge of her plate with the tines. "I read more of my mother's journal today."

"Oh? I take it you weren't happy about what you read."

She shook her head. "It made me sad to read how unhappy she was. It also made me wonder about my father. The way she describes him, he didn't show her much attention. All my grandmother would ever tell me was that he worked hard and that my mother didn't appreciate him. My grandmother never hesitated to let me know how much she disliked my mother, and she blamed her for my father's death."

Scott frowned. "I thought he was killed in a boating accident."

"When I got older, I demanded my grandmother tell me how my mother could have caused his death. She said my parents had a violent argument one night, and he left the house the next morning and never came home. Pieces of his boat later washed up onshore. She said my mother drove him to his death."

When sadness flickered in her eyes, Scott pushed his plate out of the way and crossed his arms on the table. "I'm sorry, Lisa. No matter what your grandmother thought, she couldn't be sure what happened at sea. You can't dwell on things you can't change."

She leaned back in her chair and regarded him with a questioning stare. "I can't? How about you? It seems like you can't get past what your aunt did to you."

Her words hit him like a punch in the stomach. He raked his hand through his hair. "Touché. I guess you got me on that one."

A smile pulled at her lips. "It seems we have more in common than we thought."

The better he got to know Lisa, the clearer it became they'd had very similar childhoods. After all these years, he had finally found happiness with his sisters. It troubled him that Lisa might never find that same family relationship.

He nodded. "I wish I could help you find what I have with my sisters."

She arched an eyebrow. "Have you found peace, Scott?"

"No, but I'm trying to come to grips with my past. Not just my aunt, but also the experiences I had in the military." He hesitated a moment. "Kate may have told you that I suffer from post-traumatic stress disorder. My doctors say I'm better, but I still have flashbacks."

"What kind of flashbacks?" She crossed her arms on the table, and their hands were so close Scott wanted to reach out and cover hers with his. He threaded his fingers together to keep from doing so.

"Mostly dreams. Images of my men wounded and dying. Guilt that I didn't save them. But there's one experience that's helped me get through a lot of bad days."

Her gaze roved his face. "Do you want to talk about it?"

The memory of a desert road in a faraway country flashed in his mind, but he clamped his lips together and shook his head. He'd never shared that experience with anyone, and he wasn't ready yet. "No."

"I can respect that." She leaned closer to the table. "Do you agree with your doctors that you're getting better?"

He shrugged. "Some days I think so, others I'm not so sure. I pray a lot, and I have faith God is going to be with me through all this. He's given me a family I didn't know I had. That's been a big help."

The sadness returned to her eyes. "You're lucky, Scott. I don't have any family left, and I'm afraid I lost my faith in God a long time ago."

"It makes me sad to hear you say that, Lisa. God loves you."

Lisa shook her head. "Then He's got a strange way of showing it."

Before he realized what had happened, he had reached out and grasped her hand in his. He wrapped his fingers around hers and almost gasped at the tingle of pleasure that raced through his body. He'd never before felt such an attraction to any woman as he did to Lisa, but it wasn't fair to her.

He slowly released her hand and tried to smile. "I hope I can change your mind about how God loves you before you leave the island. But as long as you're here, you know my sisters think of you as part of our family. Kate considers you her best friend, and Emma adores you. She begs all the time to come help you with the filing."

She smiled. "I love them, too. I'm really going to miss them when I leave, and I'm coming to realize how much I will miss their brother, too. You've been a great help to me these past few days."

Locking eyes with Lisa, a protective feeling surged through his soul. "Like I said, ma'am, the Ocracoke deputies aim to please."

She tilted her head to the side and studied his face. "I think it's more than wanting to please, Scott. I think you're a very kind man who cares what happens to other people. That's an admirable characteristic. And you're also very easy to talk to. Thank you for listening to me."

His heart pounded in his ears so loud that he thought she must be able to hear it. "My pleasure," he murmured.

She started to reply, but her cell phone chimed. A frown wrinkled her forehead. "That's a text coming in. Who could it be?" She pulled the phone from her purse and gasped when she glanced down at the message.

His body tensed. "What is it?"

"Oh, no!" She clamped her hand over her mouth, and the cell phone clattered to the table.

Scott scooped it up. His pulse quickened at the message displayed on the screen.

What did you think about my last visit to your

house? If you thought that was bad, wait until you see what I have planned next.

The muscle in Scott's jaw flexed. He glanced across at Lisa. Her body shook, and terror flickered in her astonished stare. Scott fought the urge to rush around the table, pull her into his arms and promise to protect her from her unseen tormentor.

Instead, he placed the phone on the table and glanced around the restaurant. The table where Ean Thornton had sat minutes ago was now empty. Everyone else in the dining room appeared to be strangers. He leaned closer and lowered his voice. "I know this is frightening, but I promise you we're going to find this guy. We'll trace this text message and find out who sent it. For now, let's get out of here."

She nodded. "I want to go back to Treasury's." She started to get up but sank back in her chair. "I forgot I left my car at the station so I could ride over here with you."

"It doesn't matter. I'm driving you to Treasury's, and I'll pick you up in the morning to go to work. Until we catch this guy, I want someone with you all the time. If I'm on patrol, then Kate or Brock need to be with you."

For a moment, he thought she would refuse. Then she nodded. "All right. I appreciate that."

He motioned for the waitress to bring their bill,

and Lisa started to pull her wallet out. He shook his head. "This is on me tonight."

"But I invited you to dinner."

"We'll do it again, and you can pay the next time."

She gave a distracted nod. "I'd like to have dinner with you again."

A panicked feeling washed through him. What was he doing? He'd promised himself that tonight would be the only time they would go out. But then he hadn't planned on a sinister text message changing his mind. He couldn't desert Lisa when she needed a friend.

He hoped he could keep their relationship on a friendly basis. She was a woman needing protection, and he was a cop. That was reason enough to be with her, but in his heart he knew it wasn't his only motive. Despite all the warning bells going off in his head that told him to keep his distance from Lisa, he realized it might already be too late to do so.

As far as he could tell, she had no idea how he was struggling against his attraction to her. If he could help it, she never would know. What he had to do was concentrate on keeping her safe until she could sell her house and move away. Then maybe he could move on, too.

SIX

The morning sun flashed a rat-a-tat message through the window of Lisa's office. The flickering patterns on the floor announced that it was another great day for sun worshippers at the beach. It might be a beautiful day outside, she thought, but a feeling of impending doom hung over the police station. Perhaps it was her imagination, or the fact that Scott had insisted she not be left alone at any time.

He had even taken his concern a step further and talked to Brock last night. They had decided the best course of action for the moment was to have an additional deputy assigned to the Ocracoke office so someone could be with Lisa at all times. That's why she was playing hostess this morning to Deputy James Clark, who had arrived on the early ferry.

Deputy Clark, one of the best-liked officers in the sheriff's department, had served Hyde County for nearly thirty years as an officer and would soon retire. Lisa had known the man all her life and always welcomed his visits to their office. However, today she wished there was no need for him to be here.

She glanced across the room to where the deputy sat hunched over another desk with his gaze directed to some papers in front of him. "Would you like some coffee?"

He looked up and smiled. "Now, don't you worry about me. I brought some reports that I needed to work on. That should keep me busy and out of your hair."

She stood and walked over to where he sat. "Deputy Clark, I really appreciate your help. I have to admit I'm a little spooked. It's hard to believe anyone could hate me that much."

His faded brown eyes softened, and he shook his head. "I've been doing this work for a long time, and I never have been able to figure people out. It seems to me folks ought to be able to get along and not hurt each other, but life don't seem to work that way." He grinned, and the wrinkles in his craggy face deepened. "I guess if it did, we wouldn't need no police officers."

She returned his smile. "I suppose you're right."

Behind her, the front door of the office opened, and she turned to see Scott entering. Her gaze dropped to his hand, which she expected to be holding a bag from The Coffee Cup. Instead, he grasped a rolled-up newspaper. He took a step toward her and stopped. "Lisa, have you seen the morning paper?"

Something was wrong. She could tell by the way he frowned and gripped the paper in his hand. She reached for it. "No. So what kind of news has Lloyd Haskell written today?"

He held the newspaper just out of her reach, and it crunched in his tightened fingers. "It's not Lloyd. Do you know a Terry Davidson?"

A tremor shot through her body at the memory of Terry's visit to the office the day before. "Yes. We grew up together and attended the island school. In fact he came by yesterday to check on me. Why do you ask?"

Scott unrolled the paper and glanced down at the front page. "Did you know he works for the newspaper?"

She gasped and shrank back against her desk as she remembered Terry's questions, which she had thought strange. "Oh, no. He knew about my mother's diary, and he asked me all kinds of questions." She glanced down at the paper. "Did he write something?"

"I'm afraid he did."

She held out her hand. "Let me see it."

Almost reluctantly, Scott passed the paper to her. "I'm sorry about this, Lisa."

The headline blazed like tongues of fire that shot

off the page and licked at her face. She tried to block the words from her mind, but they seared her brain and raced through her body— "Diary May Yield Clues to Woman's Mysterious Death."

The paper shook in Lisa's hands. Unable to speak, she glanced up at Scott and Deputy Clark. Now Terry's visit made perfect sense. He hadn't come to the police station because of concern for her. Grady had told him about the diary, and all he wanted was a story.

She shook her head in disgust. His performance had fooled her into thinking he really had come as a friend, and she had fallen right into his trap. Words that seemed so innocent at the time were now splashed across the front page of a newspaper. As soon as the locals read the account, her mother's death would be the topic of conversation everywhere.

Her hands shook, but she clutched the newspaper tighter and scanned the story underneath the headline. Each word she read made her angrier. When she finished, she crumpled the paper in her hands and jutted out her chin.

"He's despicable. The headline makes it sound like there's some big mystery about how my mother died."

"That's the hook he's using to get people to read the story, Lisa," Scott said. "The tabloids do it all the time."

"But everybody knows *how* she died. I'm probably the only one who cares *why* she died. I'll never forgive him for this," she seethed. "I can't believe he came here pretending to be an old friend, and then reported everything I said. Of course, he twisted my words to give it the slant he needed for his story."

"What do you mean?" Scott asked.

She smoothed out the front page and jabbed a finger at one line of the story. "Right here he says that I was happy to have my grandmother take care of me at night because my mother stayed at the local pub all the time. That's not what I said." Tears stung her eyes.

Sympathy lined Scott's face. "I'm sorry, Lisa."

"A-and right here…" She stabbed at the paper. "He says I'm thankful my house was broken into because it helped me find the diary that I know is going to answer all my questions about my mother's death."

He nodded. "I know. I read the whole story before I came over here."

Deputy Clark tilted his head to one side and frowned. "Don't worry about what this guy wrote. You know the truth, and it don't make no difference what other folks say. I know it hurts, but the best way to deal with things like this is to ignore it. People may talk for a few days, but something else will come along to take their minds off your troubles."

The half smile on his lips warmed Lisa's heart, and she grinned in spite of her anger. "Thank you, Deputy Clark. I'll try to remember that." She glanced at the newspaper she still held. Frowning, she wadded it into a ball, tossed it into the trash can and took a deep breath. "That's where Terry Davidson's story belongs. I think I feel better already."

Scott laughed. "Good. Now try to have a good day. I've got to get back on patrol, but there was one more thing I had to tell you."

"What?"

"I got a call from Sheriff Baxter's office, and they checked your cell phone records for that text last night. It was from a prepaid phone. It's impossible to trace an owner when it's a throwaway."

"I was afraid that might happen. I didn't think this guy would be stupid enough to use his own phone."

"And another thing… Brock told me this morning he'd gotten nowhere questioning Calvin's friends. They all have alibis. He suspects whoever broke into your house had no ties to Calvin at all."

Lisa sighed. "So that means we have no leads."

"Not yet." Scott glanced at Deputy Clark. "I appreciate Sheriff Baxter sending you over to help us out. Until we catch this guy, Brock and I think Lisa needs someone with her."

Deputy Clark nodded. "No problem. I'll stick close to her. Won't let her out of my sight."

"Good." Scott turned back to Lisa. "Do you want to do some more work at your house tonight?"

"I do, but maybe Kate could come over and help. I hate to ask you to come again."

He shook his head. "It's no problem. I'd like to go home and get out of my uniform beforehand. Can you stay here and wait for me? I get off at five, and Brock will be here until I can get back, say about five-thirty."

"I have to meet my insurance agent at three-thirty. Deputy Clark is going with me to the house, and Brock said I could forward all the incoming calls to his cell phone. I'll lock all the doors after my agent leaves, and you can come to the house when you get off work."

Scott's eyes darkened. "Lisa, I don't want you to be at home alone even for a short amount of time. It may not be safe."

The determined spirit that had often caused clashes between her and her grandmother boiled to the surface. Scott had been a big help to her in the past few days, but he didn't control her life. "I'll be perfectly fine until you get there. Don't worry about me."

Scott clenched his jaw and took a step toward her. "Lisa…"

Before he could finish his statement, Deputy Clark stepped to his side. "I tell you what. I won't leave Lisa until the insurance guy is there, but I do have to catch the last ferry back to the mainland. No telling how long her agent will be there. If he leaves before you get there, she should be okay if she locks herself in the house."

Scott bit down on his lower lip and stared at Lisa for a moment before he shrugged. "Okay, but keep your cell phone close by and call me if something seems strange. I'll come by to check on you when I make my last patrol run out to the beach."

Lisa nodded. "Okay. Now, go on back to work." When Scott had left the office, she smiled at Deputy Clark. "Thanks for helping me out. Scott has really taken his job seriously since all this started."

Deputy Clark's mouth curled into a grin, and his eyebrows arched. "From the looks of it, he seems more interested than just a deputy wanting to keep somebody safe. I'd say it's more personal to him."

Her face grew warm at the teasing glint in the deputy's eyes, and she shook her head. "No, I just think he remembers what happened to his sister when she was the chief deputy, and he doesn't want something like that to happen again on Ocracoke."

Deputy Clark chuckled. "If you say so… Now,

I'd better get back to my reports and let you get to work, too."

Lisa sank back in her desk chair and tried to concentrate on the computer screen in front of her, but it was no use. No matter how much she might try, the events of the last few days couldn't be ignored. Someone wanted her to be frightened, and she was. That wasn't anything new, though. She'd been frightened most of her life. Growing up in her grandmother's house had accomplished that.

Every person should have happy memories of childhood, and there had been times when Lisa was happy. They came on the days her grandmother was able to put aside her grief for her son who had died at sea and her hatred for the woman she held responsible. Only years later when she was in high school had Lisa realized her grandmother had suffered from depression. On the worst days her grandmother never left her bedroom, and Lisa took charge of everything. Perhaps that's what had fostered her independent spirit.

Thanks to her new friendship with Scott, those memories had receded to the back of her mind in the past few days. As much as she might protest, it made her happy to have someone who seemed to care what happened to her. She'd never felt that before, and she now realized what she'd missed in life.

Lisa pulled her attention back to the computer screen and tried to block thoughts of Scott Michaels from her mind. She had to be careful. Her feelings were beginning to chip away at her determination to keep her distance from him, and she couldn't fall into that trap. If she did, it would only lead to more heartbreak for her.

Maybe the best thing to do was to tell him she didn't want to be around him anymore, that she felt as though he was an unwelcome intruder in her life. Even as she thought it, she didn't know if she could follow through. She couldn't repay his kindness with a lie, but she had to find a way of getting the devastatingly handsome deputy out of her life.

At three-thirty that afternoon Lisa, with Deputy Clark right behind, pulled into the driveway of her house. Before she could climb from her car, Wayne Simms stopped his truck on the road in front of the house and climbed out. A briefcase dangled from his hand.

Lisa closed her car door and waited for the two men to join her. She nodded toward the deputy. "Wayne, this is Deputy Clark. He's helping us out on the island for a few days." She turned back to the officer. "And this is my insurance agent, Wayne Simms."

Wayne extended his hand. "Always glad to meet one of our county law enforcement officers."

"Just here to help Brock and Scott out for a few days." Deputy Clark glanced at his watch. "The last ferry of the day for the mainland leaves in about thirty minutes. I need to be on board if I'm going to make it home tonight. Since Lisa's had some break-ins, I need to make sure everything's all right before I shove off."

Lisa motioned for the two men to follow her. "Let's go in through the back door."

As they rounded the corner of the house, a sudden gust of wind rustled the leaves on a fig tree in the yard and rattled the wind chimes hanging on the back porch. Lisa smiled at the soothing chords emitted by the metal pipes, stepped onto the porch and inserted her key in the lock.

Another blast of air shook the house and sent two aluminum webbed beach chairs from the patio blowing across the backyard in opposite directions. "Oh, no," she gasped. "I'd better get those before they blow away."

She jumped from the back porch with Deputy Clark right behind. "I'll get the one on the right. You get the other one," he called out.

Lisa sprinted to the back of her property and grabbed the chair. "Got it," she yelled.

Deputy Clark with his chair in tow approached from the side of the yard. "Here's the other one."

She headed toward the house, where Wayne still stood on the back porch. The wicker swing hanging at one end swayed in the wind. She'd spent many peaceful moments there reading and listening to the wind chimes. Her gaze moved to the small patio, and she recalled cookouts with Kate and her sisters. Why did those happy memories come back now when she was about to put the house up for sale? She sighed and shook her head. She'd made up her mind a long time ago to sell, and her burglar hadn't forced her to change her decision. Now she needed to get to work so that she could move on.

"Lisa, your telephone's ringing." Wayne's voice cut through her thoughts.

"That's okay. I have an answering machine."

Wayne pushed the door open. "I don't mind getting it." He stopped and glanced over his shoulder. "Hey, I smell gas in here."

Before she could protest, Wayne rushed into the house. She took a step toward the house, but a blaze of light followed by a deafening boom jolted her backward. A heavy weight slammed against her, knocking her to the ground and sucking the breath from her body. Something pinned her to the ground, and she gasped for air. Her eyes widened in shock at the realization that Deputy Clark's limp body covered hers. He didn't move.

Her ears rang, and she blinked her eyes. She lay on her back staring upward over the officer's shoulder. Above, the sun lit the blue clouds that floated by as on most afternoons on Ocracoke, but something was very wrong today. She pushed at the law officer, and he groaned. Blood trickled from a jagged wound on his head. Again she pushed, and he tumbled onto his back, his eyes closed.

Scrambling to her knees, she leaned over the unconscious man and checked the pulse in his neck. He was alive, but she had no idea what kinds of injuries he had sustained. With her heart banging like a bass drum, she pushed to her feet and stared in incomprehension at the pile of rubble scattered across the area where her house had once stood. Only a few concrete blocks marked the foundation of the home that had been built by her great-grandparents.

Nausea rose in her throat, and she wrapped her arms around her waist. In panic she scanned the yard for Wayne. Where was he? The memory of a ringing telephone and his last words ripped through her body and left a trail of unbelief in its wake. She sank to the ground next to Deputy Clark's prone figure. With trembling fingers she reached into her pants pocket for her cell phone.

Her eyes wouldn't focus on the phone's keypad. She blinked and rubbed her hands across her eyelids to clear her vision. Squinting, she held the phone at eye level and punched in the number for the island emergency services. Deputy Clark was badly injured, and she had to get help for him. For

Wayne, though, there was nothing anyone could do. Sorrow flooded through her as she grappled with the enormity of the loss. He, along with her house and all her possessions, had evaporated in an instant. She didn't know what had caused the explosion, but nothing that had happened to her up to this point could compare with the fear that now consumed her.

SEVEN

Scott Michaels, ready for a short break, glanced at his watch and frowned as he pulled into the parking lot at the police station. What was Brock's cruiser doing in its usual space? He wasn't scheduled to come on duty for another hour and a half. Then Scott remembered Brock had said something yesterday about paperwork he needed to get to Sheriff Baxter. Maybe that's what had brought him in early.

As he climbed from his car, he thought of Lisa and wondered how her meeting with her insurance agent was going. They should be at her house right now. He smiled at the thought of spending the evening with Lisa again. Even though the hours he'd spent with her came under the heading of official business, he'd enjoyed their time together. Lisa put him at ease, and he'd never felt that before.

Lost in thought, he stepped onto the porch of the police station. At the moment he reached for the doorknob, a sound like a sonic boom split the air. He whirled, ran back to the parking lot and scanned the sky for black smoke. He'd heard enough explosions in the military to recognize that sound. Something big had blown up.

Then he saw the smoke. A black cloud rose high into the afternoon sky. He shaded his eyes and tried to determine the location, but it was no use. Suddenly his lapel mike crackled. "Ten eighty at 100 Oyster Road. All EMS respond."

For an instant Scott froze. An explosion at Lisa's house? He tried to make his legs move, but it was no use. It was as if his body had turned to stone.

The mike squawked again. "Possible 10-54."

Now his legs went limp, and he braced his hand against the side of his car. A dead body? With the other hand he grabbed at his chest. His lungs burned as if all the air had been sucked from his body. He didn't think he could move, but his survival instinct born of battle experiences kicked in. He lunged for the car door and jumped inside.

Lisa. Lisa. Her name blazed through his head as if it rotated on a blinking sign. He had promised he would protect her. Had he failed her as he had the men in his command?

The door to the police station burst open, and Brock ran to his cruiser. "Scott," he yelled over his shoulder. "Get rolling to Lisa's house." He pulled the door to his car open and frowned at Scott, who still hadn't pulled out. "Now!"

Scott shook his head to rid it of the horrible memories of death and destruction raging in his mind. He'd seen enough carnage to last a lifetime. Now he had to face what might possibly be the worst ever—another person who'd died because of his failure.

He took a deep breath, gunned the engine and roared out of the parking lot with the siren blaring. Tourists stood on every village street pointing at the cloud of smoke that now drifted toward the shoreline.

As he'd done so many times before, he pulled up the memory and focused his thoughts on it. *Remember the lamb. Remember the lamb.* The words echoed through his mind.

He skidded onto Oyster Road and raced behind Brock's car toward Lisa's house. At the end of the road he saw an ambulance and fire trucks. The car slid to a stop, and Scott was out before the engine died.

"Please, God," he prayed. "Let Lisa be all right. I don't want to see her dead or injured like so many in my past. Please…"

The spot where Lisa's house had stood looked like a battlefield. Remnants of the cottage and its furnishings lay scattered across the front yard and to the rear of the property. Deputy Clark's and Lisa's smoke-stained cars sat in the driveway. Flying debris had shattered their windshields and dented the cars' bodies. Scott's stomach roiled at the sight of the destruction.

Several volunteer firemen from the island station huddled around the yard, and two of the EMTs he had come to know stood at the back of the open ambulance. He raced after Brock toward the men.

When they reached the vehicle, Scott hesitated before approaching the men. He didn't want to ask about casualties. He couldn't. What if Lisa lay on a gurney inside the vehicle either dead or dying? How could he ever cope with that?

"What happened?" he heard Brock ask.

Arnold Tucker, one of the EMTs, turned toward them. "All I know is that the house exploded. One victim was inside at the time."

"Who was killed in the explosion?" Scott tensed for the answer to Brock's question.

"An insurance agent named Wayne Simms," Arnold answered.

Brock glanced somberly at Scott. "He's got a wife and two kids." He turned back to Arnold. "Anybody else hurt?"

Arnold pointed to the inside of the ambulance. "One of your deputies was hit by something during the blast. We're about to transport him to the health center."

"Can I talk to him?"

The EMT nodded, and Brock climbed into the back of the ambulance.

Scott inched forward. No one had mentioned Lisa yet. "Wh-what about Lisa Wade, the owner of the house? Was she hurt?"

Arnold shook his head. "No, she was at the back of the yard when the house exploded." He pointed to a pickup truck on the other side of the ambulance. "That's the fire chief's truck. She's sitting inside. I think she's finished with her statement to him."

Scott closed his eyes and exhaled. *Thank You, God, for sparing her life.*

He stepped to the back of the ambulance and peered inside. Brock bent over the still form of Deputy Clark. "Brock, Lisa's in the truck on the other side of the ambulance. Do you want to question her, or would you rather I do it?"

Brock's ashen face mirrored the anguish Scott felt. "You go on. I'll be there in a minute."

Arnold stepped up beside Scott and placed his hand on the door. "Deputy Gentry, we have to go now. You can talk to Deputy Clark as soon as Doc says it's okay."

Brock squeezed the deputy's arm and jumped to the ground. He inclined his head toward the truck. "Go on and talk to Lisa, Scott. I see the fire chief across the yard. I'll check with him first."

Scott nodded and walked around to the passenger side of the fire chief's truck. Before he could open the door, it swung open and Lisa tumbled out.

Scott barely had time to reach for her before she wrapped her arms around him and began to sob. He closed his eyes and tightened his arms around her trembling body. There had been other times when he'd offered comfort to battle-scarred victims, but he'd never experienced the protectiveness he now felt for Lisa. All he wanted was to hold her in his arms until her fears vanished.

"Scott," she wailed, "I've never been so scared in my life."

She buried her face in his shoulder, and he raised his hand to stroke the back of her head. "Shhh, Lisa. You're all right now. Brock and I are here. We'll take care of you."

She drew her head back and stared into his eyes. "Did you hear about Wayne? He was in the house when it exploded."

She began to cry again, and Scott eased her head back to his chest. "Don't think about that now. I'm thankful you're alive. I prayed all the way here that you were all right."

A hiccup shook her body. "You prayed for me?"

"Yes."

She pulled back, and her gaze searched his face. "No one has ever told me they prayed for me. I'm glad you were the first."

Unable to pull his eyes away, he stared down at her. "I am, too."

In that moment, Scott knew his relationship with

Lisa had passed the point of being classified as a friendship. Something deeper had developed. It was still too raw and new to put a name on it, but whether he wanted it or not, it had happened.

After what seemed an eternity, she released her hold on him and took a step backward. His arms drifted to his sides. His skin that had burned with heat a few seconds before now felt cold. All he wanted was to hold her in his arms, but the highly charged moment had been broken.

She pushed her hair out of her eyes and glanced past him. "Where's Brock?"

Scott cleared his throat and pulled a notepad from his pocket. "He's talking with the fire chief."

The piercing wail of the ambulance siren split the air. They watched the vehicle with Deputy Clark inside speed down the road. Lisa's eyes filled with tears again. "H-how is Deputy Clark?"

"I don't know. The EMTs didn't give us any details. There are a lot of unanswered questions right now we need to know. Can you tell me what happened?"

For the next few minutes, he wrote as she related the events that led up to the moment the house exploded and sent deadly missiles of debris flying across the yard. He paused when she started to cry again. "Deputy Clark was unconscious, and I pushed him off me. Then when I stood up, I realized Wayne had been inside the house. He's married to one of my friends from school. What will she do?"

Before Scott could answer, Brock walked up. "Hi, Lisa. How are you doing?"

She wiped at her nose with a tissue she pulled from a pocket. "As well as anybody can in a circumstance like this, I guess."

A sad smile pulled at Brock's lips. "We're thankful you weren't hurt. I've called Kate. She's coming to take you to Treasury's house."

"Thanks, Brock."

"Have you given Scott your account of what happened?"

"I have, but what did Chief Wilson say? Why does he think my house blew up?"

He glanced at Scott and back at her. "We may never know for sure, but he has a theory."

Scott leaned closer. "What is it?"

"He said you told him Wayne heard the phone ring and opened the back door you had already unlocked. Is that right?"

Lisa nodded. "I yelled to him and told him I had an answering machine, but he said he smelled gas. The next thing I knew the house exploded."

Brock took a deep breath. "Chief Wilson said if there was a gas leak in the house, any number of things could have set it off, including a spark from a ringing telephone."

Scott shook his head. "But Lisa and I were here

last night, and there wasn't a gas leak then. Do you think this could be related to everything else that's happened to Lisa in the last few days?"

Brock shrugged. "I don't know at this point. I guess we'll have to find out."

Lisa faced the pickup truck, propped her elbows on the fender and buried her face in her hands. "This is a terrible nightmare. First I have my home invaded and vandalized, and now there's a man dead. Nothing can be worse than that."

Her cell phone chimed, and she pulled it from her pocket. Her hand shook as she stared down at the screen. "What is it? Scott asked.

"It's a text." She raised her head, and her gaze locked with his. "It just got worse."

Scott had seen fear on grown men's faces many times in his life, but nothing had ever equaled the terror that darted across Lisa's face. He reached for the phone. "Let me see that."

She stared at him a moment before she released the phone. His fingers curled around it, and he read the cruel message that almost pulsed on the screen. *Watch your back. I'm closer than you think.*

Pursing his lips, Scott handed the phone to Brock. He wished he could wrap Lisa in his arms as he had done minutes before, but he didn't move. In the last few minutes, the stakes had risen to a new level. He was no longer looking for a burglar.

Now he was on the hunt for a killer.

* * *

Hours later, Lisa sat on the back porch and sipped the glass of lemonade Treasury had fixed for her before she retired for the night. The elderly woman never ceased to amaze her. She cooked and cleaned all day and never seemed to tire of all the upkeep required to keep the big Victorian dwelling that housed her bed-and-breakfast in shipshape condition. She would be up early in the morning to begin another day by preparing a big breakfast for her guests to eat at the wicker tables arranged on the big wraparound porch.

Now with no home, no car and only the few belongings she'd brought with her to Treasury's a few days ago, Lisa had little in the way of worldly possessions. Somehow tonight it didn't matter. Over the last few days she had come to see how blessed she really was. Treasury had opened her home to her, Kate had calmed her after the house explosion and Scott had been by her side most of the time.

She snuggled back in the big wicker chair and drew her feet up under her. A warm feeling flowed through her body at the thought of Scott. A few days ago she'd felt he was aloof and unfriendly. Now she'd seen another side of him. There was a lot more to the real Scott than he let other people see. She had caught a glimpse of a caring human being, and she liked what she saw.

A car's headlights blazed in the driveway as

someone drove to the back of the bed-and-break-fast. Lisa sat up straight and half rose from her chair, ready to run if necessary. She breathed a sigh of relief when Scott's car came into sight.

He pulled to a stop and headed toward the back door. The oil lamp on the table cast a glow across his chiseled features as he stepped onto the porch. Lisa suppressed a gasp at how handsome he looked, still in his uniform, even after a rough day.

"Hello, Scott."

He whirled in surprise. "Lisa, I didn't see you. What are you doing out here?" His eyebrows arched, but that didn't disguise the fatigue that lined his face.

"I'm having some lemonade. Can I get you some?"

He dropped into a chair opposite her and smiled. "No, thanks. Brock and I've been over at the health center with Doc, and I wanted to check on you before I went home."

Lisa pushed the glass of lemonade away and crossed her arms on the table. "How is Deputy Clark?"

"They've airlifted him to a hospital on the main-land. Doc thinks he'll recover all right, but he needed to be at a facility that could offer better care than his emergency setup."

"I'm glad to hear that."

Scott shifted in his chair and clasped his hands

on top of the table. Her heart fluttered at how near he was. She could almost reach out and touch him. He glanced from her to his hands and pulled them back to his lap.

Her cell phone on the table beside her rang, and she glanced at the number before answering. "Hi, Jeff."

"Lisa, are you all right? I just saw on the news that your house blew up!"

She winced and pulled the phone away from her ear. "Calm down, Jeff. I'm fine. Where are you?"

"When I got off work this afternoon, I took the ferry to the mainland. I'm in Swan Quarter tonight, but I'll be home in the morning when I bring back Travis Fleming's boat. But I'm worried about you. Do you need anything?"

She chuckled. "Everything I have is gone, Jeff, but I'm fine. I'm at Treasury Wilkes's bed-and-breakfast."

"Good. I won't worry about you then. And I'll see you when I get back tomorrow."

"See you then. 'Bye, Jeff."

She disconnected the call and glanced at Scott. He stifled a yawn. "Is there anything I can do for you before I go on home?"

She wanted to ask him to stay longer and keep her company, help her drive away the fears that had filled her mind for the last few days. But he was tired, and he had to be at work early. She shook her head. "No, but thanks for coming by."

He pushed the chair back and stood. "I'll come by and take you to work in the morning."

"Okay."

The muscle in his jaw jumped, and she wondered if he was going to say something else. After a moment, he gave a curt nod. "Good night."

She caught up with him before he got to the first porch step and touched his arm. "Scott."

He whirled to face her, and she gasped before she released her hold on him. The wild-eyed glare he directed at her sent chills down her spine. It reminded her of a savage tiger she'd once seen in a zoo. The animal had growled and pawed at his cage in anger at being trapped. The freedom he wanted was out of his reach. Now Scott Michaels looked at her as if he shared that animal's fate.

"What is it, Lisa?"

She wanted to thank him for praying for her today, but the words froze in her throat. She shook her head. "Nothing. I'll see you in the morning."

Without a word he rushed down the steps and to his car. She watched the lights disappear down the driveway before she blew out the oil lamp on the table and walked into the house. Something she didn't understand had bothered Scott. She racked her brain for what she could have done to offend him. Then it came to her. She had fallen into his arms when she had first seen him at her house.

Lisa rubbed her hand across her eyes and groaned. She shouldn't have done that, but she was so frightened at the time. It had seemed so natural to seek comfort from a friend.

Her face grew warm at a new thought. Maybe Scott thought she'd wanted more than friendly support. If he'd interpreted it as a plea for a romantic involvement, she'd have to apologize. She'd told herself over and over romance was the last thing on her mind. It still was, she insisted, even if that brief moment had shown her in his arms was exactly where she wanted to be.

She clenched her fists at her sides and gritted her teeth. She needed something to take her mind off Scott Michaels. Her mother's journal. She'd put it in her purse before leaving the station. That was what she needed to distract her.

Lisa hurried upstairs and into the bedroom that for now was her home. Her heart skipped a beat when she pulled the diary out. If she had left it at her house, it would be in shreds now. She rubbed her hand over the smooth cover and sank into the chair by the window.

She forced the events of the day from her mind and opened the book to the spot she'd quit reading the night before. Those entries had left her disturbed because they portrayed a woman who grew increasingly desolate as the months went by. According to her mother's entries, she had followed through on her desire to escape her unhappy life. Night after night she had left the house for the Sailors' Catch after her mother-in-law had gone to sleep. Lisa's heart ached for her mother's unhappiness.

It still didn't seem real that these were her mother's words, but they were. Lisa pressed the book open and began to read the next entry.

August 15, 1982.
I haven't written anything in weeks, but now I must share my thoughts with someone. Since there is no one I can trust, I have no choice but to write them down. The life I've hated will change soon. Not in the coming weeks, but sometime in the future. It's all because he came into my life. Even for you, dear diary, I can't speak his name. There are reasons it can't be shared now, but in time to come everyone will know. I never thought I could love like this, but he has brought a joy to my heart that makes me want to sing. My mother-in-law must suspect something because I catch her staring at me. She pretends to care about me now because I'm expecting a child.

But little does she know that the child I carry
is not her son's. The father is he whose name
I guard in my heart.

The journal tumbled from her lap as Lisa sprang
to her feet. She pressed her fist against her mouth
to keep from screaming. This couldn't be happening. Not to her, the daughter of a respected island
fisherman who had died at sea.

Lisa stared at the book for a moment before she
reached down, picked it up and reread the entry.
She had wanted to know her mother better, to understand the woman she'd never known, but she
hadn't wanted this. No one should have to read
such horrible revelations.

She wondered why she wasn't crying. This warranted tears, but she had none to give. Earlier she
had checked off a mental list of the personal belongings she had lost in the last few days—her
house and its furnishings, her clothes and her car.
None of that seemed important compared to what
had just been taken away from her. Her name,
her identity—everything that had bound her to a
family and a home had vanished.

She walked to the dresser and stared into the
mirror. The blond, blue-eyed girl she'd always been
stared back at her. "Who am I?" she whispered.

The image in the mirror had no answers.

EIGHT

Scott steered the cruiser through the village traffic. This morning he couldn't concentrate on his job, which was unusual for him. A deputy never knew what to expect on Ocracoke patrol. With all the tourists on the island every day during the summer, anything could happen. Scott had hoped there would be at least be enough activity this morning to keep him busy. Nothing major, just something to keep his thoughts off Lisa and all that had transpired between them.

He hadn't slept. Every time he closed his eyes, her face popped into his head, and he was wide awake again. He'd never been so confused in his life. When he'd held her in his arms after the explosion, it had felt so right. But it wasn't. He'd promised himself he wouldn't become attracted to a woman. It could only lead to hurt for both of them.

The thought of how they'd parted the night before made him groan. At the time all he'd wanted was to get away from her before he said or did something he'd regret. The way she looked at him made him want to pull her out of that chair and kiss her. But that wasn't about to happen, not if he could help it.

This morning when he'd driven her to work, she'd barely spoken. The air conditioner couldn't have made the car any chillier than it had been on their short ride. She'd rushed into the station as soon as they'd arrived and had begun to prepare for the day's work, all the time completely ignoring him. He was glad the new deputy had arrived from the mainland, and he could concentrate on filling him in on his assignment to be with Lisa.

Scott guided the car into the parking lot at the police station and pulled to a stop. He dreaded going inside, but he wanted to see how she was doing. After a moment he climbed from the car and walked inside. Lisa glanced up and without any greeting got up and walked to the break room at the rear of the station.

Jason Lewis, the temporary officer, looked up from the desk where Deputy Clark had sat yesterday. Scott winced at the memory of the older man lying in the health center. "Have you heard any news about Deputy Clark's condition this morning?"

The young man stood and stretched. "Sheriff Baxter called about fifteen minutes ago. He said he'd regained consciousness, and the doctors think he's going to be okay."

"That's good news."

"Yeah." Deputy Lewis closed the file he'd been working on and yawned. "I hate sitting around like this. It makes me sleepy. Why don't you stay here for a while, and I'll take patrol for you?"

Scott glanced at the break room, but he couldn't see Lisa in there. "Sure. Do you know the route?"

"Yeah. I pulled some duty over here before they hired you. I know my way around Ocracoke well."

Scott tossed him the keys to the squad car. "Thanks. Enjoy your ride."

He grinned. "I will."

Scott waited until Jason had left the office before he walked to the break room. He stopped at the door and peered at Lisa, who sat on the small couch at the back of the room. Her hands covered her face, and she leaned forward with her forearms resting on her knees.

"Lisa, are you all right?"

She jerked to a sitting position and wiped at her eyes. "I'm fine."

He took a step closer. "You don't look fine. What is it?"

She pushed to her feet. "I don't want to talk about it." She clenched her fists at her side and strode toward the door.

Scott couldn't let her go like this. He propped his arm across the doorway to block her exit. "Wait a minute."

She gritted her teeth and glared at him. "Please get out of my way."

Scott's eyebrows arched at her icy tone. Their parting the night before flashed in his mind yet again. Could she be upset with him because she realized how he wanted to get away from her? If he was the reason for her anger this morning, he needed to do something about it.

"No, I won't get out of your way. Not until you tell me what's bothering you. I know you're upset over your house and the text message, but I get the impression it has something to do with me." A muscle twitched in his jaw. "Have I done something to offend you?"

She slumped against the doorframe as if all the air had gone out of her body and pressed her hands to her temples. "I can't take much more of this, Scott."

He took her by the hand and guided her to the couch, then eased down next to her. "We're going to catch this guy, Lisa. I promise you. And we're going to see that you're safe."

Her eyes glistened with unshed tears. "I appreciate that, but I don't know what you can do. Nothing has stopped him yet."

"Lisa, I told you I'd protect you…and I will."

She shook her head. "You can't put your life on hold to watch after me. I don't want to impose on you anymore."

He sucked in a breath. If he could only tell her how much he wanted to be with her. "You haven't imposed on me."

"Yes, I have. While I'm at it, I want to apologize for falling into your arms yesterday. I didn't mean to act like a silly female. I'm sorry I did that."

"I'm not." The words were out of his mouth before he realized it.

Lisa cocked her head to one side and stared up at him. "You're not? But after the way you acted last night, I thought you were angry with me. I didn't want you to think that I have designs on you or anything like that. I needed a friend at the time, and I thought we were friends...."

The scent of her perfume filled his nostrils and sent a longing he'd never known rippling through his body. He might tell himself that he wasn't going to get involved with a woman, but his heart told him he'd already passed the point of no return in his feelings for Lisa.

He reached for her hand and cradled it in both of his. "I acted like a jerk last night, Lisa. I should have been more understanding of what you'd gone through." He paused for a moment and took a breath. "I still have trouble dealing with my past. I come with a lot of baggage, and I wouldn't wish that on any woman, especially you."

She smiled, and his heart did flip-flops in his chest. "I have my own demons, Scott. Right now, there's someone who's taken away everything I've owned in this world. And the worst part is, it looks like he wants to take my life, too."

Scott squeezed her hand tighter. "I'll never let that happen."

"When you left last night, I went to my room and began to feel sorry for myself because of what I'd lost—my house, my car, my possessions, and I thought your friendship. I didn't see how things could get any worse, but they did."

"What happened?"

Her lips trembled. "I should have listened to you about the journal. You said I might not like what I found."

"I only wanted to protect you."

She sniffed. "I know, but I didn't listen. I read my mother's diary, and I lost the last thing I had that was mine. I lost my name."

He frowned and shook his head. "I don't understand."

A tear trickled from the corner of her eye. "I found out that my mother had an affair while she was married. My father wasn't John Wade. It was someone else."

For a moment he couldn't speak. Lisa's face crumpled into a mask of despair, and in her eyes he saw a hurt similar to the one he'd experienced since childhood. He put his arm around her, drew her head to his shoulder. He turned his mouth to her ear. "People often say they know how you feel when something happens to hurt us, but in this case I understand," he whispered.

"You do?"

"A year ago a private detective found me in San Antonio and told me I had three sisters who had been looking for me. I'd never known who I was until that moment. I grew up not knowing anything about my father. Since I've been here, I've come to know him through the stories my sisters tell. I know how much it hurts to have a piece of your life missing. I don't want that for you."

She raised her head and stared at him. "What are you saying, Scott?"

"I'm saying let's concentrate on our first priority now—finding out who wants to hurt you. Then I'll do everything I can to help you find out who your father is."

Her eyes lit up. "You will?"

He nodded. "I will."

Lisa returned her head to his shoulder and snuggled against him. "Scott, will you do something else for me?"

"What?"

"Will you come to Treasury's house tonight and be with me when I read the next entry in my mother's journal?"

His grip on her tightened. "If that's what you want."

"It is."

"Then I'll be there."

She released a long sigh. "Thank you for being my friend."

Scott's heart fluttered as Lisa's words flowed over him like a soothing ointment. This latest revelation had forged a new bond between them. Both of them suffered deep wounds inflicted by adults who let their selfish desires interfere in the lives of the children they should have protected.

Years ago, she had lost her mother and the man she thought was her father. Now that she knew the truth, she could have other family she'd never known. Maybe even somebody who lived on Ocracoke. He'd found his family, and it had answered all his questions about his true identity. He wanted answers for her, too.

As he'd said, though, first they had to find out who wanted to silence her forever.

Lisa wiped her mouth on her napkin and laid it on the wicker table beside her plate. Dinner on Treasury's back porch tonight had been more enjoyable than sitting in the big dining room with all of the inn's guests. Across from her Scott sipped his iced tea and stared off into the distance.

"What are you looking at?"

He set the glass down and straightened in his chair. "The sky. I've never seen so many stars in my life."

She gazed up at the twinkling dots in the night-time sky. "Ocracoke is a haven for people who like to do stargazing because there's nothing obstructing their view."

Scott chuckled. "Yeah. When I first came here, I could hardly believe there wasn't a traffic light in the village and very few streetlamps. You don't need a telescope to get a view of God's handiwork."

She picked up her fork and placed it on her plate. "Speaking of God, I want to thank you again for praying for me when the house blew up."

He pushed his plate out of the way and crossed his arms on the table. "I pray for you all the time, Lisa."

Her eyebrows arched. "You do?"

"Praying for my friends and family every day is natural for me. Isn't it for you?"

She shook her head. "No. I've never had much time for religion. My grandmother didn't believe in God. She said all that Bible stuff was a bunch of superstition."

"I'm sorry she felt that way. I don't know how I could have survived everything that's happened to me if I didn't have my faith to keep me going. I've been in situations before that I couldn't control. All I could do was turn it over to God and put my life in His hands."

"Are you talking about some of your battle experiences?"

His forehead wrinkled, and he ground his teeth together for a moment before he answered. "Yes."

"Do you want to talk about it?"

He took a deep breath, and she waited for his response. "Not now…"

She reached across the table and squeezed his arm. "You've helped me so much, Scott. If I can ever do the same for you, I want you to know all you have to do is ask."

He stared down at her hand. "I'll remember," he whispered. "Some things I've never been able to talk about to anybody but God. Maybe I'll be able to talk about them someday."

"You two need anything else?" Treasury's voice called from the back door.

Lisa jumped up and gathered their dishes. "No, thanks. You outdid yourself tonight."

Treasury grinned and stepped onto the porch. She pulled the bottom hem of her apron up and wiped at the perspiration on her forehead. "Aw, go on now. It wasn't nothing special."

Scott chuckled and followed Lisa to where Treasury stood. He stopped and put an arm around the elderly woman's stooped shoulders. "Every meal I eat here is special, Treasury."

She reached up and patted Scott's face. "It's always my pleasure, son."

Treasury's face beamed, and Scott kissed her on the cheek. "You're the only one who's ever called me son. It sounds sweet coming from your mouth."

Lisa bit down on her lip and hurried past the two

into the house. She knew Scott's sisters loved Treasury like a mother, and now he did, too. Her heart ached with the need to have someone care for her as Treasury did for the Michaels family.

No one had ever called her their daughter either, but maybe someday they would. If only her mother's journal would give her a clue where to start looking, she might find her father. Or like Scott, some siblings.

When she returned minutes later with the diary in her hand, Scott stood in the downstairs hallway. He pointed toward Treasury's office at the back of the house. "Treasury said we could sit in there. There may be guests in the parlor."

She clutched the journal tighter and preceded him into the small room. Lisa had never been in the office before, and she scanned the sparse furnishings. A desk with a computer on it sat facing the door, but it was the couch that caught her attention. A long, padded foam cushion formed the seat of the sturdy wooden frame, and decorative throw pillows graced the back. Pictures of lighthouses up and down the Eastern Seaboard sat on the desk and a table, and what appeared to be an antique barometer hung on the wall.

Scott closed the door behind them and followed her to the sofa. When they were seated, she leaned back against the pillows and took a deep breath. "I'm almost afraid to look at the journal again."

"You don't have to, you know."

"Oh, yes I do if I want to find out who my father is."

He reached out and squeezed her hand. "I'm right here with you, Lisa."

Her hand shook as she opened to the page she had marked the night before. She thumbed through the next dozen or so pages before she looked up. "Her next entries are short, some just a few sentences. They almost look like they were written in haste."

She began to read aloud, and soon her suspicions were proven right. According to the short notations, her mother was having trouble keeping the diary a secret from her mother-in-law, who hovered around her all the time. Most of the hastily jotted messages told of quick meetings with "him" at the lighthouse, which now was their regular meeting place because it had become too dangerous to be seen together. "He," she wrote, had persuaded a park ranger friend of his to give him a key to the tower so they could meet in secret.

She turned a page. "Here's one that's dated two weeks after I was born.

"March 30, 1983.
John left on the boat this morning, and my mother-in-law went to the village. It was the first time I'd been alone since Lisa's birth. I

still can hardly believe the happiness I feel every time I look at her. The door opened, and he walked in. It was the first time he'd seen his daughter, and I've never seen so much love on anyone's face. He held her and kissed her until I was sure her face would be chapped from his lips. He only stayed a few minutes, but it was enough just to see him. He promised that soon we would all be together. Before he left, he gave me a gift—a beautiful, silver-framed hand mirror. It looks as if it might have cost a lot of money at one time, and the diamond-swirled initials E. D. engraved on the back make me suspect the mirror came from the *Elena.* I didn't ask because all I care about is that he said he was giving the mother of his child something that would make me think of him when I looked into the mirror."

Lisa blinked back tears. "At least it sounds like she and my father, whoever he was, loved me."

Scott smiled. "I'm sure they did, Lisa. It's not your fault that their lives were such a mess."

A distant memory tugged at her thoughts, and she frowned. "That mirror he gave her made me remember something."

"What?"

"At night sometimes when I'm lying in bed it's almost like I can hear a man's singsong voice crooning. It says, 'Lisa is a pretty girl.' When I close my eyes, I can visualize a mirror in front of my face. I wonder if that was my father and if the mirror belonged to Elena."

Scott, who'd been leaning against the cushions, sat upright. "Elena? Who is she?"

"From the stories I've heard, her name was Elena Dinwiddie. But I don't think my mother is referring to the woman. It's the ship that was named for her."

"I've never heard of the ship. What do you know about it?"

Lisa searched her memory for the story she'd heard the islanders talk about all her life. "Back in 1922, during a big storm the remains of a ship washed up on Diamond Shoals. It was the *Elena* out of Maine. It was on a return voyage from South America with a full cargo hold and a fortune in money for the goods sold down there." She took a breath. "It took several days for the storm to die down enough so that anybody could board it. When they did, there was no one on board and all the cargo was gone. But they did find a note stuck in a bottle in a cabinet in the galley."

"What did it say?"

"It said that pirates were about to board the ship."

Scott's eyes grew wide. "Was that the truth?"

Lisa shrugged. "No one ever found out what happened to the *Elena*. It's still a mystery today."

Scott leaned back. "Wow! Pirates and a ship missing its crew, money and cargo. That sounds like something that might have happened when Blackbeard sailed these waters."

She chuckled. "Yeah, but by that time he'd been dead for two hundred years." She stared back at her mother's words. "But how would my mother have thought that mirror had come off the *Elena?* That shipwreck happened over thirty years before she was born."

Scott thought for a moment before he jumped up, hurried to Treasury's computer and sat down in the desk chair. "Hey, why don't we look up the *Elena* and see what we can find?"

Lisa hurried over to stand behind him. "I think they have an exhibit about it over at the Graveyard of the Atlantic Museum on one of the other islands."

Scott typed the name in the search engine and navigated to the site. Lisa leaned over his shoulder and stared at the page that displayed photos of the battered ship on the beach. He pointed to an article at the bottom of the page. "Look at this. It says there are several theories about what really happened aboard the ship. One is that crew members mutinied and divided up all the valuables on board. Then they rowed ashore in lifeboats, leaving the boat to sink. The other one is that rumrunners who actively smuggled liquor along the Eastern Seaboard during the days of Prohibition boarded the ship, robbed it, then killed the crew."

Lisa walked back to the couch and sank down. Pirates and rumrunners? What possible connection could her mother have to people like that? The cushion next to her dipped, and she knew Scott had eased down beside her.

"Lisa, what's the matter?"

"First I find out my mother was an unfaithful wife. Then I discover she has some connection to thieves and murderers. I think I've opened Pandora's box, Scott. It would have been better if we'd never found that diary."

He put his arm around her, and they leaned against the couch's cushions. A few days ago she'd been filled with excitement that she was about to start a new life somewhere else, but those feelings had vanished in a downpour of violence and heartbreak.

If it would ease her fears, she would grab the few clothes she had left and board the ferry to the mainland tomorrow. But that wouldn't help. Her unknown assailant might follow her. Then what would she do? In another place, there would be no one who cared enough to help her. At least here she had a strong support system.

Leaving would have to come later. For now there

were too many unanswered questions. Two unknown identities tied her to this island. One belonged to her biological father and the other to a killer. The revelation about her father had taken away the name she loved. The other person wanted to take her life. She couldn't leave until she discovered the names of both.

NINE

The thoughts that had kept her awake half the night drummed in her head the next morning as she sat at her desk. Across the room Deputy Lewis glanced at his watch every few minutes. With a reputation as one of the most aggressive lawmen in the county, he had to hate his assignment of playing nursemaid to a police dispatcher. Thanks to Brock and Scott, however, Sheriff Baxter had agreed she needed someone with her at all times.

She smiled in his direction. "Have you heard from Deputy Clark this morning?"

He glanced up from his paperwork and nodded. "I called in while I was on the ferry. They said at the station he'd had a good night and might get to go home today."

"That's good." At least Deputy Clark survived. Her heart still ached for Wayne Simms and his family. She stared into space. "They're having a memorial service today for Wayne at the church he attended in Greenville when he was growing up."

"I heard one of the ferry workers talking about that. They said his wife was really taking his death hard," Deputy Lewis mumbled.

Lisa glanced at him and winced. He looked absorbed in the papers before him and probably didn't have a clue that his brief reply had pierced her heart. He couldn't know that she blamed herself for Wayne's death. It would have been better if she'd run into that house ahead of him to answer the phone. At least she wouldn't have this terrible guilt.

The front door opened and jerked her thoughts back to the present. Travis Fleming strode in and headed toward her desk. She hadn't seen the island's most successful businessman in weeks. Travis might be in his mid-forties, but he looked years younger. He pulled his Oakley sunglasses off and propped them on his head.

"Good morning, Travis. What brings you to the sheriff's office today? I hope you don't need help from the police."

A frown wrinkled his brow. "I was on my way over to the marina to meet your cousin, who's bringing one of my charter fishing boats back from the mainland this morning, and thought of you when I drove by the station. I thought I'd take a few minutes to stop in and let you know how sorry I am about all the problems you've had."

"Thank you, Travis. It's good to know I have

friends who care." Deputy Lewis had glanced up when Travis first entered but now appeared to be ignoring them. Lisa balled her fists and pushed to her feet. Jason Lewis might not care how she felt, but there were still people like Travis who did. She needed to remember that. "I appreciate you stopping by more than I can ever tell you."

He stuck his hands in his pockets and shook his head. "I can't believe there's someone on this island who would be malicious enough to break into your house and then try to kill you, according to Grady, by blowing up your house."

She sighed at the mention of Grady Teach. "There are no secrets when Grady gets involved."

He chuckled. "You're right about that." He frowned again. "Is there anything I can do to help you? If you need money for anything, I hope you know you can come to me."

Suddenly a thought struck her. "Do you have time to talk to me for a minute or two?"

He glanced at his watch and nodded. "It should be another fifteen minutes or so before Jeff gets to the dock."

"Deputy Lewis, will you cover my desk for a few minutes?" she called over her shoulder as she led Travis to the break room. They settled on the couch, and she took a deep breath. "Did you know my f-father worked on one of your father's boats when I was born?" She couldn't believe how hard it was to refer to the man she'd always believed to be her father.

His forehead furrowed as if in thought. "I may have heard that at one time, but I really don't remember. How long ago was it when your father died?"

"Nineteen eighty-six."

"I was in school at the University of North Carolina then. I really didn't know a lot about my father's business. My grandfather was still active in it at that time. Why do you ask?"

"I was only three when both my parents died, and I want to know more about them. I know your father lives on the mainland now, but I wondered if he could tell me anything about my father."

He shook his head regretfully. "I'm afraid not. I moved him to what I told everyone was a retirement home some years ago. That's true, except that it's a facility that specializes in the treatment of Alzheimer's."

"Oh, Travis. I'm so sorry. I had no idea."

He took a deep breath. "It's nothing to be ashamed of, but somehow I didn't want the people who'd always thought him to be such an active man to know what his life is like today."

"I understand."

His eyes lit up. "But maybe I could find something in the business records about your father and the boating accident."

"That would be great."

He glanced down at his clasped hands and then back up at her. "I read in the newspaper about your mother's diary. Does your interest in your father have something to do with that?"

"I suppose it does. Like I said—I need to know more about my parents."

He exhaled and stood. "Well, I can understand that. I'll see what I can find out." He reached in his pocket and pulled out a business card. "In the meantime, here's my card. My cell phone number is on there. If you need anything, Lisa, give me a call."

"I will."

She walked with him to the front door and smiled as he walked out. There really was no other place like Ocracoke. Here neighbors helped each other and cared what went on in their lives. She probably would never find that again.

Scott's face appeared in her mind's eye. She wouldn't find anyone else like Scott either. Her heart fluttered at the thought that she'd be with him again tonight for Treasury's birthday party. It would give her a chance to observe him surrounded by the sisters who had searched for him, and would also let her see how he had adjusted to life in the house where he now lived with two of his sisters. She wanted to see how families should love each other.

Her face grew warm, and she pressed her hands to her cheeks. What was she thinking? The love that the Michaels family had for each other wasn't something she was ever going to experience. Secrets from the past had insured that. She needed to put some distance between her and Scott before she began to wish for things that could never be. But until the killer was caught, she wouldn't be able to do that.

Scott stacked the dessert plates containing the remains of Treasury's birthday cake and followed Betsy into the kitchen. With the last present opened and dessert served, a comfortable peace had settled inside him and he smiled.

"What are you smiling about?"

He stopped beside Betsy at the sink and handed her the dishes. "I was just thinking how good it feels to be here with all of you. I don't ever remember celebrating anybody's birthday like this."

She set the dishes in the sink and brushed a stray lock of hair out of her eyes. "Didn't your aunt make a big deal of your birthday when you were little?"

He shook his head. "Nope. Just another day, she'd say. I don't think she ever gave me a present. Of course, she bought me stuff all the time, like clothes and school supplies. But somehow it never seemed right." He sighed. "Even when I was little,

I knew I didn't belong with her, but I didn't know where I was supposed to be."

She leaned with her hip against the sink and bit her bottom lip. "I say this all the time, but I'm really so sorry about all you missed out on with us."

He leaned over and kissed her on the cheek. "Me, too, but we're making up for it now, aren't we?"

She smiled and nodded. "We are indeed, especially since you've moved in with Emma and me. I wanted Kate and Brock to have a place of their own, but I wanted to keep this house. It makes it perfect having you here now."

"I love it, too. But then, I like everything about the island."

At that moment, Lisa's laughter rang out from the direction of the living room, and Scott glanced over his shoulder. When he turned back, a mischievous grin pulled at Betsy's mouth. "So, you're loving everything about the island? I thought it might be a special someone who has made you seem happier for the past week."

His face reddened. "I know you're talking about Lisa, but we're just friends."

"You haven't acted like she's a friend."

"What do you mean?"

Betsy sighed. "The way your eyes light up when

you look at her sends a signal that you think she's the most beautiful woman in the world."

Scott raked his hand through his hair and exhaled sharply. "I didn't realize I was being so transparent. I'll have to do something about that."

Betsy reached out and touched his arm. "It's all right, Scott. You deserve to have some happiness, and Lisa is one of our best friends. She's perfect for you."

He shook his head. "No one's perfect for me," he growled.

Betsy's eyes grew wide, and she straightened to her full height. "What are you talking about?"

His hands shook, and he grasped the back of a kitchen chair to steady himself. "You don't know what I've seen, Betsy, or what I've done either."

She placed her hand on his and squeezed. "You still can't lay your battle experiences to rest, can you?"

"No," he whispered. He clenched his jaw and stared at her. "I've killed people, Betsy. How can I ever get past that?"

Tears pooled in her eyes. "You aren't a murderer, Scott. You served your country and did what was expected of a soldier. You can't live the rest of your life blaming yourself for what happened in battles where you were trying to stay alive and keep your men safe."

"But there were so many I couldn't save. I still hear their voices in my head."

"You may always hear their voices, but there's one you need to listen to more than those. It's God's voice. He loves you and wants you to live again without guilt about the past."

Scott took a deep breath. "I know that, and I'm trying."

She smiled. "He's started you on the road to recovery by bringing you here to a family who loves you and wants to help you." She glanced toward the living room. "And he's given you a chance with a woman who seems to be as interested in you as you are in her."

He chuckled and shook his head. "Now you're trying to placate me. Lisa doesn't care anything about me. She's going to leave this island as soon as we catch the guy who's been terrorizing her."

Betsy tilted her head to one side. "Oh, I don't know about that. I noticed during dinner she kept watching you all the time. Maybe you aren't picking up on her signals."

"Signals? Are you serious?"

Betsy laughed and looped her arm through his. "Oh, Scott. I see you need the expert guidance of your sisters when it comes to understanding a woman's feelings." She pulled him toward the door. "Let's go back in the living room, and you ask Lisa to take a walk on the beach with you."

He shook his head. "She'll turn me down."

"You think so, huh? Ask her and see. If she agrees to go, I'll fix all your favorite foods for dinner for the next week."

The playful glint in Betsy's eyes warmed his heart. Having three sisters in his life was the best thing that had ever happened to him. Maybe Betsy was right. God didn't expect him to carry this guilt with him forever. He had to try to move on in his life even if he met with disappointments. Asking Lisa to walk on the beach might not seem like a big deal to some men, but to him it was as scary as a baby taking his first steps.

He smiled. *Baby steps.* That's what he had to do. Take one step at a time. He squeezed Betsy's hand that rested on his arm. "Okay, sister, let's go see what she says."

Scott's burst of courage fizzled when he walked into the living room. Treasury sat on the sofa between his sister Kate and Lisa, whose gaze appeared fixed on the small box in her hands. She glanced up at Scott. "These earrings you gave Treasury for her birthday are beautiful, Scott. You have great taste."

Her face glowed in the room's soft light, and he thought he'd never seen anyone more beautiful. "Thank you," he mumbled.

She placed the box back on the coffee table and

smiled. "Remind me to let you know when it's my birthday. I like earrings, too."

His Adam's apple bobbed up and down, but he couldn't speak. Betsy's elbow punched him in the side, and he cleared his throat. "I'll do it." He took a deep breath. "Lisa, I was thinking I might take a walk on the beach. Would you like to join me?"

She frowned. "I'd like that, but I really need to help Betsy and Kate with the dishes."

Kate pushed to her feet and propped her hands in the small of her back. "I'll help Betsy. The baby gets restless if I sit too long. You go on with Scott, and we'll take care of the kitchen."

Lisa jumped up. "Are you sure you're up to it?"

Kate laughed. "Lisa, I'm having a baby. Women do it all the time." She waved her hand in dismissal. "Now, go on and enjoy this nice evening out on the beach." She glanced at Scott. "Take the flashlight on the table beside the door. It's dark out there this time of night. I've shown you the spot where Brock and I like to sit and enjoy God's handiwork. Take Lisa there."

He nodded. "I will."

Lisa grinned and headed for the door. "Then let's go."

Scott picked up the flashlight and glanced over his shoulder before he followed Lisa onto the front porch. Kate and Betsy stared after him, smiles on their faces. "Come on, Kate," he heard Betsy say.

"I have to make a grocery list. It seems like I'll be cooking Scott's favorite foods for a while."

He shook his head and grinned as he pulled the door closed. Lisa waited in the front yard. The light from the house lit the way toward the dune ridge beyond the sandy yard. However, once they stepped onto the beach, darkness enveloped them. Scott flicked on the flashlight, and the beam lit their way.

The splash of waves breaking on the beach drifted on the night air, and Scott guided Lisa toward the sound. "Want to wade in the surf?" he asked.

Lisa giggled joyously. "I haven't done that in years, but it sounds good."

They pulled off their shoes and inched closer until the rolling water lapped at their feet. Scott grasped Lisa's hand, and they walked in silence along the shoreline. After a few minutes, he guided her away from the water and to a spot farther back on the sand. "Let's sit here. Brock and Kate come here a lot to listen to the sounds of the night and watch the stars."

They dropped down on the sand. Lisa propped her arms behind her and leaned back to gaze into the sky. "It's so beautiful here. Sometimes I wonder why I want to leave. I'll never find another place like this."

He nodded. "I never expected to find a place like

this. Now that I'm here, I doubt if I'll ever leave." He hesitated a moment. "Maybe you'll change your mind and stay."

"Maybe," she whispered.

With that one word, Scott's heart soared. Could Betsy be right? Was Lisa interested in him? Then the reality of all the unanswered questions in Lisa's life hit him. As soon as she found out who wanted to kill her and who her father was, she would leave. If he didn't watch out, he'd be left behind with a broken heart.

"I know you'll make the right decision."

She sat up straight and groaned. "I've had a wonderful time tonight, Scott. So great that I almost forgot what's happened in the last few days. But I can't let myself forget. I have to remember."

She began to sob, and he put his arm around her and pulled her closer. "I know how you feel. Betsy and I were talking in the kitchen earlier about my past. She told me that God didn't want me to dwell on things that had happened to me, and He wants you to be happy, too, Lisa."

She shook her head. "How can I be when I feel so guilty for Wayne's death? It's my fault he's dead."

"You're not responsible for that. Brock thinks whoever did this broke into your house before you arrived and turned the gas on full blast hoping you'd come home and be asphyxiated. Wayne just happened to be there when the house exploded."

The tears flowed from her eyes. "But don't you see, Scott? Wayne gave his life for me. How can I ever repay his family for that?"

He took both her hands in his. "Again it seems like our lives are similar. I've felt like that so many times in the past. God has been telling me I'm not to blame for all the men who died around me, but I haven't really listened to Him. It's the same with you." He released a deep breath. "You don't have to repay Wayne's family, Lisa. You have to do the same thing Jesus tells me every day. You have to live your life so it would honor His death. God wants you to be happy, Lisa."

The tears on her cheeks sparkled in the moonlight, and he wiped one away from underneath her eye with his thumb. Her lips trembled as his thumb grazed her skin. "Do you think God really wants me to be happy, Scott?"

"I know He does. Just like He does for me."

Her eyebrows pulled into a frown. "But you still can't put the memories of the past to rest, can you?"

He stared at the waves rolling onto the beach and tried to say the words he knew God would want him to speak. "I still have problems, Lisa, but that's not God's fault. For right now, I'm thankful for the strength He gives me to face each day. He doesn't push me to hurry. He just waits for me to come to the point I can give it all up to Him."

"When do you think that will be?"

He shrugged. "I don't know. I've come a long way, but He's not through with me yet."

"I wish I could have faith that God wants to help me," she whispered.

"But He does. All you have to do is ask Him. God loves you, Lisa. I'd like for you to come to know Him."

She stared at him for a moment. "Thank you, Scott. Maybe we can talk about this again sometime."

He took her hand and pulled her to her feet. "We will. Now I think it's time we went back. Everybody will be wondering where we are."

They walked hand in hand across the beach. As they came closer to the house, he wished their time together didn't have to end. It felt so good to have Lisa beside him. A year ago he'd thought finding his sisters was all he could ever wish for, but now there was a new desire in his heart. It focused on the woman beside him.

TEN

Lisa hummed as she walked down the stairs at the bed-and-breakfast. Ever since waking this morning, her attitude had been more upbeat than it had in days. She stopped about halfway down and leaned against the banister. Her good mood might be a result of the talk she and Scott had on the beach the night before.

His words had touched her and made her realize other people had bad things happen to them. Something else had happened on that beach, too. Her attraction to Scott had moved into another realm. What she might have once considered infatuation had crossed over into a much deeper feeling.

Lisa hopped down the rest of the steps and hurried to the kitchen in hopes there was something left from breakfast. She came to a halt at the kitchen door and stared in shock at Scott sitting at the kitchen table drinking a cup of coffee.

He set his cup in the saucer and grinned. "It's about time you got up. Treasury went outside, but she said if you hadn't come down by the time she got back, she was going to roll you out of bed."

She swallowed her surprise, strolled to the coffeemaker and poured herself a cup. Easing into the chair across from him, she took a sip and closed her eyes. "Umm, that's good. You need to know I'm not very talkative until I've had my first cup of coffee. But what are you doing here on a beautiful Saturday morning?"

He crossed his arms on the table in front of him and shrugged. "Since neither one of us has to work today, I came to ask you to go somewhere with me."

"Where?"

"I thought we could visit the Graveyard of the Atlantic Museum over on Hatteras. I saw online that they have an exhibit about the *Elena*." He glanced at his watch. "If we hurry, we can catch the next ferry."

She leaned back in her chair and cleared her throat. "Scott, I appreciate that more than you'll ever know, but you don't have to spend your free time trying to help me find out about my past."

"I want to spend my time helping you. Truth is, I like spending time with you."

Her heart fluttered, and she smiled. "I like spending time with you, too. I'll go get my purse."

She started to get up from the table, but he pointed to her cup. "What about your coffee? I don't want to spend the day with a cranky woman who won't talk because she didn't get her caffeine fix."

She laughed, picked up the cup, and chugged the contents. Setting the cup in the saucer, she murmured, "Taken care of. I'll see you in a few minutes."

Lisa dashed from the kitchen and took the stairs two at a time to the top. In her room, she rushed to the mirror and checked her makeup, then twisted and turned to study her reflection. The shorts and tank top she'd put on looked perfect for the excursion. She turned to leave but glanced back and smiled. The color in her cheeks wasn't from the powder blush she'd applied earlier. It came from the surge of happiness that shot through her body at Scott's words. He liked spending time with her.

She liked being with him, too, even though she knew it might lead to heartbreak later on. Today she didn't care. She and Scott had both had their share of bad times in the past. They deserved to have some fun, and today that was just what she wanted to do. She was going to enjoy being with this man who made her feel so incredibly special.

Scott opened the car door for Lisa and waited for her to climb out. The afternoon sun reflected off the ocean waves that rippled onto the beach across the street from the museum. He glanced at the white building dedicated to honoring the history of the Atlantic and the ships that sailed it.

Several monuments about exhibits inside the building dotted the museum parking lot, and Scott let his gaze drift over them. Lisa adjusted her sunglasses and stared out to sea. "It's beautiful, isn't it?"

"Yeah." He took her hand, and they started toward the entrance, but he stopped next to one of the stone markers. He read the inscription on the sign and gave a low whistle. "Have you ever heard of the *Monitor?*"

She nodded. "Yes. It was on its way to Beaufort when it got caught in a windstorm and sank."

He glanced back at the words engraved on the monument. "Yeah, in 1862. This says the *Monitor* is one more treasure that the ocean hides." He nodded toward the ocean. "There's no telling what's buried out there beneath those waves."

Her gaze followed his to the rolling waves. "That's why they call it the Graveyard of the Atlantic. The man I called my father is out there somewhere. His body was never recovered."

Scott tightened his hold on her hand. "Come on. Let's go in and see what we can find out about the mysterious *Elena*'s fate."

Inside the building, hushed voices of visitors greeted them. Small groups of people moved from one exhibit to another across the high-ceilinged entry. Sunshine from the large skylights overhead lit the room.

Lisa pointed to a sign on the wall. "This says the exhibit about the *Elena* is down this corridor."

They stepped around a family who huddled in front of the *Monitor* exhibit, and headed toward the other end of the hallway to the glassed-in area that told the story of the *Elena.* They stood without speaking as they each read the story of the doomed ship whose mysterious tragedy had never been solved.

"The story told here is exactly the same as what you told me," Scott said.

Lisa pointed to a picture of a woman at the christening of the ship. "The caption under this picture says this is Elena Dinwiddie after breaking a bottle of champagne on the bow of the ship. Look at the scarf she's wearing."

Scott leaned forward and studied the long scarf that circled her neck and hung down to her waist. The swirled, monogrammed letters *ED* were visible on the scarf. "She's a very pretty woman." A gasp escaped Lisa's mouth, and he turned to stare at her. "What is it?"

Her eyes appeared locked on something behind the glass, and she pointed a shaking finger. "Look at the back of the hand mirror, Scott. It has the same letters that are on the scarf. This has to be the mirror my mother wrote about in her journal."

She whirled to face him. "But if she had it, how did it get here?"

A woman wearing a name tag that identified her as a museum employee walked down the hallway, and Scott stopped her. "Excuse me. I wonder if you could answer a question for us."

The woman smiled. "I'll try. My name is Susan, and I'm one of the exhibit designers here. What would you like to know?"

Scott pointed to the mirror inside the case. "Can you tell us about this mirror?"

Susan's gaze drifted over the mirror. "Isn't it beautiful? There's quite a story behind that piece. When the ship washed up onshore, the manifest was still intact in the captain's cabin. It had a detailed listing of everything on board. One of the items mentioned was a silver-covered hand mirror with Elena Dinwiddie's initials in diamonds on the back. It was a birthday gift the ship's owner, Hiram Dinwiddie, had made for his daughter in Rio, and it was being brought back on the voyage." She paused briefly then continued. "Over the next few weeks after the ship beached, items that had been on board washed up onshore, and they were checked off against the recovered manifest. But the mirror didn't show up, and everyone assumed it was at the bottom of the ocean."

Lisa frowned. "I don't understand. How come you have it now?"

Susan smiled. "About twenty-five years ago Elena Dinwiddie, who was an elderly woman at the time, received a package in the mail. It didn't have a return address, but it had been mailed from Ocracoke Island. When she opened the box, the mirror was inside. When she died, the mirror passed to her granddaughter, and she thought it needed to be included in the exhibit. She sent it to us about a year ago when we moved the museum into this new building."

Lisa stepped closer to the glass and studied the diamond-swirled initials on the back of the hand mirror. "It's a beautiful piece."

Susan nodded. "Yes, it is. We're fortunate it didn't end up at the bottom of the sea."

Scott spotted the slight tremor in Lisa's body, and he grasped her hand before he directed his attention back to the museum exhibit designer. "I'm new to Ocracoke, but I've heard the story of the *Elena.* What do the employees here think? Did the crew really commit mutiny, or do you think the ship was boarded by rumrunners?"

"We really don't know. Of course the shipwreck happened during the Prohibition era, and the Eastern Seaboard was a haven for smugglers trying to get alcohol into New York. That's why they were called rumrunners. A lot of them resorted to piracy of unsuspecting ships." She shrugged. "I doubt if we'll ever know whether or not that was the *Elena*'s fate or if it was a mutiny. Then again, it could have been a storm that did her in."

Lisa turned a pleading look toward Scott. He had to get her out of here before she burst into tears. He smiled to Susan. "That's an interesting story. Thank you for sharing it, but we need to leave."

"Without seeing the rest of the exhibits?" Susan's eyebrows arched. "There's a lot more farther down the hallway."

"I know, but we'll have to come another day. Thanks again."

Without waiting for the woman to question them further, he pulled Lisa toward the exit. When they walked into the sunshine, she gulped a deep breath of air and bolted for the car. He caught up with her just as she opened the door.

"Lisa, are you all right?"

She whirled to face him, her fists clenched at her side. "How do you expect me to be all right?" The words spewed like sharp barbs from her mouth. "In the past few days, I've been attacked, my home blew up, I found out I have a father I never knew about, and now this—my mother was tied in some way to the mystery behind the *Elena*."

"We don't know that about your mother, Lisa."

"How can you say that?" she cried. "You saw that mirror. It's the same one she had. It's the one I remember somebody holding in front of my face. My mother must have sent it to Elena Dinwiddie."

"That's a logical explanation, but we still don't know anything for sure. Even if it is true, we don't know why she would send it."

Lisa patted the large purse hanging from her shoulder. "I stuck the diary in here before we left Ocracoke. I think the answer is in it. Can't we go somewhere and read it? Try to find out how my mother came to be in possession of that mirror? The answer may lead me to my father."

Scott nodded. "All right, if that's what you want. But nothing in that journal has brought you happiness yet. I'm afraid you may not like any other answers you discover."

She blinked at the tears filling her eyes. "It's too late to worry about that now. I don't have a choice... I need answers."

He reached around her and pulled the car door open wider. "Okay. Get in. We'll find somewhere quiet to sit so that we can read what comes next."

Lisa bit her lip and climbed into the car. Scott stared at her a moment before he closed the door and headed toward the driver's side. He wished he had never found that journal. Lisa needed to concentrate on who had tried to kill her, not on events that transpired when she was a child.

He sighed and shook his head. There was no use thinking like that. He knew from firsthand experience how unanswered questions about your past could block everything else from your mind.

As long as she wanted answers, he would help her. He only hoped it wouldn't wind up hurting her instead.

Fifteen minutes later, Lisa and Scott sat at a picnic table in a shaded park across the street from the beach. Lisa stared at the families who played in the rippling surf with their children. A child's laughter rang out, and Lisa smiled. A little girl sat on her father's shoulders as the two walked into the water.

"I wonder what it's like?" she said.

Scott glanced at her. "What?"

"To spend time with your father."

He pushed to his feet and jammed his hands in his pockets. "I wouldn't know."

A pang of regret sliced through her, and she touched his arm. "Of course you don't know. I guess we're alike in that way." She pointed to the child and her father in the water. "Neither one of us ever had what that little girl is enjoying right now. She doesn't realize how lucky she is."

"No, she doesn't." Scott rubbed the back of his neck and sat down. "Why don't you get out the journal and let's see if we can find any answers about the mirror?"

Lisa pulled the book out of her bag and opened it to the spot she'd marked. "I've read everything up to this point. Most of it is about day-to-day stuff.

There's a lot about me and how I'm growing, and she writes a lot about how much my father loves me. She said at one point that he wanted to get a divorce, but his wife refused."

"So he kept your mother thinking he was going to marry her, even though you were three years old at the time?"

"That's right. Maybe he never intended to get a divorce."

Scott's hand closed over hers. "Lisa, no matter what happened between the two of them, you need to remember that your mother said he loved you."

She tried to smile, but her lips trembled. "I'm trying to think that way, but it's hard." She glanced down at the page. "Well, this looks like it may be the last entry. Let's see what she wrote."

"Do you want me to read it for you?"

"No. I can do it." She took a deep breath and then forged ahead.

"I haven't written in several weeks, but I can't keep this to myself any longer. The truth about the *Elena* has almost driven me mad. Who would have thought a shipwreck that happened before I was born could ruin my life? When he told me the truth, I thought I could live with it, but I can't. I mailed the mirror back to the real owner today. I hope it arrives safely. He told me I shouldn't have done that.

He's afraid they might try to trace it, but they won't be able to find out anything. But he's not the one I fear. It's the evil one who hates me and wishes I was dead. Lisa is three years old, and I can't keep silent any longer. For her sake, I have to stand up to them. Tomorrow everyone on the island will know who Lisa's real father is. Nothing matters now except that Lisa is recognized as his child. I don't regret anything I have done. It's all been for my sweet Lisa. Someday she will be a very rich woman."

Scott's eyebrows arched. "Is that all?"

"Yes, it's her last entry. The date at the top of the page is the day she died. So, at some point during that day she planned to tell everyone who my real father was, but instead she committed suicide. Why would she do that?"

Scott appeared to be mulling that over. The muscle in his jaw flexed, and he took a deep breath. "Your mother said there was someone who wished she was dead, but she indicates it's not your father. Maybe she didn't commit suicide after all."

Lisa gasped and jumped to her feet. "Oh, Scott, you don't think…"

He nodded. "Her words don't sound like a woman who's desperate enough to commit suicide. Maybe she was murdered."

Lisa sank back down on the picnic-table seat. All these years she'd wondered why her mother didn't love her enough to stay with her. Could it be possible she and everyone else on the island had been wrong?

Her body shook, and a rage as hot as molten lava bubbled up in her heart. No, everyone hadn't thought her mother committed suicide. One person knew the truth because he had murdered her.

She threw her head back and moaned. "No! No! No!"

Scott gathered her in his arms and pulled her close. "It's all right, Lisa. We'll get through this."

She buried her face in his shoulder. "How could anyone do that? I wish I'd never seen that journal."

Even as she cried out her anguish, a resolve was forming in her mind. Somebody on Ocracoke knew who her father was, and she intended to find him. Then the next step would be to track down the person who had killed her mother. Maybe then she would find answers for all the questions that had haunted her all her life.

ELEVEN

Scott always enjoyed Sundays, but this one had already exceeded his expectations. As he exited the small church he attended with his sisters, he lifted his face to the sun and soaked up the rays shining down from the cloudless sky. The preacher's sermon had been one of the best he'd heard, but that wasn't what excited him today. For the first time since he'd been on the island, Lisa had joined him and his sisters for Sunday-morning worship.

He touched her elbow to guide her down the three steps in front of the church, and she smiled at him. "Thank you for inviting me this morning. I really enjoyed it."

"Good. Maybe you'll come with us again." She appeared happy this morning, and he hoped the service had given her something to think about.

She glanced back at Betsy, Emma and Kate walking out of the church. "I'd like that. It's very peaceful here."

Emma raced down the steps and caught up with

them in the parking lot. "Lisa, are you coming to our house for lunch?"

Lisa cocked an eyebrow and smiled. "Why? Are you cooking?"

Emma giggled and shook her head. "No, but Kate and Betsy want you to come, too."

Scott put his arm around his little sister and faced Lisa. "And my vote makes four who want you to come. Brock is going to come by on his lunch break. So the whole family will be there. How about it?"

Her mouth twisted into a grin, and she cupped Emma's chin in her hand. "I'd love to eat with the Michaels family."

Scott smiled. "Good. And after lunch we can take a walk on the beach."

"I'd like that."

He glanced down at Emma. "You want to ride with us or Betsy and Kate?"

Her eyes sparkled. "I want to ride with my big brother."

"Then it will be my pleasure to accompany two lovely ladies to the Michaels' home for lunch."

Emma grabbed Lisa by the arm, and they hurried across the parking lot to his car. He stood still a moment watching them. The little sister he loved dearly and the woman who was slowly working her way into his heart. Was he being honest with her by continuing to see her?

The last thing he wanted was to make her think there might be something in the future for them. Try as he might, though, he couldn't stay away from her. Now with the new revelations about her parents, she needed someone even more. He had to be there for her as long as she wanted his friendship.

An hour and a half later, Lisa and Scott spread a blanket on the beach and plopped down onto it. Lisa threw her head back, closed her eyes and listened to the waves rippling near her feet. "Umm," she murmured. "The salt water smells good today. I've always loved the beaches on Ocracoke. I'm really going to miss being near the water."

Scott picked up a handful of sand and let it sift through his fingers. "Do you know where you're going after you leave here?"

"Not yet, but I'm thinking about somewhere in the mountains of western North Carolina. I visited there once and thought it was beautiful country."

He nodded. "Yeah, it's different from the beach."

They sat without talking for a few minutes before Lisa spoke again. "I don't know when I'll go. I'd like to have some questions answered before I go."

"You mean about your father."

"Yes."

He took a deep breath. "You may never find

the answers you want. I wouldn't have found my family if they hadn't looked for me."

She gave a snort of disgust and pushed to her feet. "Yeah, and my father knew about me. If he's still living, he's kept his secret well hidden for twenty-eight years."

Scott hopped up beside her. "I'm sorry, Lisa. I didn't mean to hurt you."

She rubbed her head. "It's okay. I'm still trying to cope with all this."

Scott opened his mouth to respond, but instead chuckled. "Well, would you look at that."

Lisa turned and laughed at the sight of Grady Teach walking along the beach with a metal detector in his hand. He moved slowly and scanned the surface as he moved closer.

Lisa cupped her hands around her mouth and called out, "Hey, Grady, what are you doing?"

He grinned and came to a stop beside them. "What I do every day. Looking for treasure."

Scott pointed to the metal detector. "It looks like you have the right equipment. Found anything lately?"

He shook his head. "Nope. There's too many others on our beaches now. Not like it was when I was growing up. I don't know what's happening to my island."

She smiled at the reference to *his* island. "Sometimes I don't either."

He shifted the metal detector in his arms, repositioned his straw hat on his head and pushed his long hair out of his eyes. "Yep, it's a new day on Ocracoke. Tourists crowd the streets, and there are bicycles everywhere. Not like when I was growing up."

Lisa nodded. "But we're thankful for the tourists and all the money they bring to the island."

"Yeah, I guess so, but it's hard to get used to. It's different than when we were just a little fishing village on one of the barrier islands. Folks here cared about each other back in the old days, and we all worked hard." He shook his finger at Lisa. "Now, take your daddy and his brother, for instance. They never had time for drinking and taking drugs like the foolishness we see nowadays. They was too busy learning a trade so they could make money to live on."

Lisa's skin prickled at the mention of her father and his brother. Why hadn't she thought of talking with Grady before? He might remember something that could help her search for answers to the mystery in the journal. "You knew my father and his brother well when they were growing up, didn't you?"

"Yep. Back in those days I knowed everybody living here."

"And you knew my mother, you said."

He grinned. "Yeah. Prettiest woman ever lived on this island. You look a lot like her."

"I don't remember her," she murmured. "Can you tell me anything about her? I know she was lonely when my father was gone. Did you ever see her around the island?"

"Oh, yeah. Back in those days I hung out at the Sailors' Catch nearly every night. There was always a bunch there, and you could always find a friendly game of cards. I remember your mama used to come two or three times a week. She'd get there late, and the fellers would tease her that she had to wait until her warden went to sleep."

Lisa cast a glance at Scott, and he shook his head. "Lisa, I don't think…"

Before he could finish, she cut him off. "Did she have any particular friends she met there?"

Grady tilted his head to one side, closed an eye and tapped his temple. "Let me think. Everybody liked her, especially the men. She was the prettiest woman we'd ever seen around here."

Lisa leaned closer. "But was there someone she seemed to like better than anyone else?"

Grady grinned. "Oh, yeah. There was one feller who was head over heels in love. Couldn't stay away from her even though he knew she was married."

Lisa's heart pounded. "Who was it?"

"Ean Thornton."

Lisa tried to keep from gasping. "You mean Mr. Thornton who lives in the big Victorian house with the gingerbread trim? The one whose son Mike received a life sentence for the murder of Jake Morgan?"

Grady nodded. "Yep, that's the one."

Lisa took a deep breath and tried to steady her trembling legs. "Thanks for telling me about my mother, Grady. I appreciate it."

"Glad to do it." He glanced at his watch and arched his eyebrows. "I didn't know it was getting so late. I've got a full afternoon taking tourists on walking tours around the village. See you two later."

As he hurried down the beach, Lisa turned to Scott. "Did you hear what he said? Ean Thornton could be my father."

Scott shook his head. "Don't get too excited, Lisa. Just because he liked your mother doesn't mean he was your father."

"But it's possible."

Scott took her hand in his. "I know you want to find your father, but I have to tell you I hope it isn't Ean."

Her eyes widened. "Why?"

"You've worked at the police station enough to know why. He's always thought Kate harassed his son when she was chief deputy on the island. He even accused her of making his life so miserable that he committed murder because of her. He hates my family."

"I know."

"Then you also know that the only thing he cares about in life is his son who's in prison. He hasn't stopped trying to get his conviction overturned."

Tears pooled in her eyes. "But he could be my father."

Scott held up a hand to silence her. "If he is, you'll be better off not knowing. The man is a bully and a tyrant. Nobody can get along with him. You know how many complaints come in every week to our office from someone who's had a run-in with him." He grasped her arms and stared into her face. "I don't want you to get hurt. You need to stay away from him."

She squared her shoulders and bit her lip. "I can't make any promises."

Scott released her and scooped up the blanket from the beach. "I hope you know what you're doing."

Turning, he walked toward the dune ridge next to his house. Lisa didn't move but let her gaze drift over his retreating figure. His slumped shoulders sent a message of disappointment, and it pricked her heart.

She clenched her fists at her side. He should

understand how she felt. After all, he'd found his family. That's all she wanted to do—find the man who was her father. If she could do that, she might finally have all the pieces of her life that could bring her the peace she craved.

Monday mornings were always busy, but Lisa thought this one seemed even worse than usual. She hadn't even had time for a break. In a way she was glad. Being busy meant she didn't have time to think about her conversation on the beach with Scott yesterday.

She had been so upset when she got back to the bed-and-breakfast that she'd read and reread her mother's journal. Then last night when she'd put it away, she spotted something in the drawer she had ignored earlier—a Bible. Treasury placed them in all the rooms, but Lisa hadn't opened the one in her room since she'd been at the bed-and-break-fast. Her visit to church had told her something was missing in her life, and she felt drawn to read about God.

By the time she got ready for bed, God's word had begun to seep into her soul, and she knew she'd taken the first step in allowing God into her life. In contrast, she feared her disagreement with Scott yesterday might have taken her a step away from him.

She still smarted from his words about Ean

Thornton. She'd known the man all her life, and she knew he had a reputation as a difficult man. But what if he was her father? If he was, that would make a relationship with Scott impossible. Until she knew the answer to her question, she needed to reevaluate her friendship with Scott.

A cough across the room startled her, and she glanced at Deputy Lewis, who'd arrived on the ferry early this morning. "I'm sorry you have to babysit me again. I know you'd rather be working on the mainland today."

He shook his head. "No problem, but I doubt if I'll be able to do it much longer."

"Why not?"

Deputy Lewis pushed to his feet and stretched. "I stopped by the sheriff's office this morning before I went to the ferry. Sheriff Baxter told me they've been trying to track down some new meth labs operating in the county. It looks like he's going to pull me off of Ocracoke to work on that problem."

Lisa chewed on her bottom lip and nodded. "I'd heard about the increase in meth-related arrests, and I understand why you're needed there. I've enjoyed having you here, but I can't say I'm sorry to see you go. I really don't think I need somebody with me every minute."

Deputy Lewis shook his head. "Sheriff Baxter

likes you, Miss Wade, and he's concerned about your safety."

She waved her hand in dismissal. "I'm sure Scott and Brock have had something to do with Sheriff Baxter's concern, but don't worry about it. I'll be fine. I just hope you and the other deputies are able to track down those meth dealers. I know how drugs can ruin a person's life."

"Oh?"

"My cousin." She let out a sigh. "My grandmother spent a lot of money to send him to rehab, and I'm still not sure if it worked."

"That's too bad." He wriggled his shoulders again. "Man, I'm getting stiff from sitting so long. I'm looking forward to getting back in action."

She grinned. "I must say I'm thankful we haven't seen too much action while you've been here."

He glanced at the clock. "Hey, it's almost lunchtime. Scott should be here any minute. When he comes in, I'll go on patrol for him. That'll give me a chance to get out."

Lisa sat back down at the computer. "I wish he'd hurry up. He's supposed to bring me something for lunch, too, and I'm beginning to get hungry."

Fifteen minutes later, Scott walked through the door, two sacks from the Sandwich Shop in his hands. "Man, it's getting hot out there."

The temperature outside had to be in the eighties today, but she couldn't tell it by Scott's appearance.

His uniform looked as crisp and fresh as it had when he'd picked Lisa up earlier for work. With his ramrod-straight posture and muscular toned body, she could imagine his picture on a poster as the perfect example of what the military expected in recruits.

She shook the thoughts of how handsome he looked out of her mind and pointed to the sacks he held. "I hope one of those is for me."

He nodded and held one out. "I'm still aiming to please, ma'am."

She laughed and glanced at Deputy Lewis. "What about you, Jason? I'll share my sandwich with you."

He shook his head and pushed to his feet. "I'll take over patrol while you two eat." He put his hat on and checked the revolver on his service belt. A mischievous smile pulled at his mouth as he headed for the door. "Besides, I've always heard three's a crowd, and I wouldn't want to interfere with two lovebirds spending some time together."

Lisa's cheeks flamed. She opened her mouth for a retort, but the door banged behind him. She glanced up at Scott, and he appeared as shocked at Jason's words as she was. She grabbed the sack Scott still held and sank down in her chair.

Her fingers fumbled at the top of the sack, and she thought it would never open. When she pulled out her sandwich, she glanced up at Scott, who still stood beside her desk. Neither one of them had spoken.

Scott clutched the other sack in his hand and stared at her. The look in his eyes scared her. What was it? Anger at Jason's words? Or regret that he might have made her believe he had feelings for her? Or could he be angry because her problems had interfered with the quiet life he had fashioned for himself here in Ocracoke with his sisters? She cleared her throat and tried to smile.

"I thought I'd stay at my desk while I ate. Do you want to drag up a chair and sit with me?"

His mouth thinned into a straight line, and he shook his head. "No, thanks. I think I'll go in the break room so I can relax on the couch."

Her heart dropped to the pit of her stomach. His words hit her like a slap in the face. She directed her attention back to the sandwich as she picked it up. "Okay. Have a nice lunch."

He strode to the back room, and with every footstep her heart pumped a little harder. She shouldn't have worried about a relationship between Scott and her. The look of panic on his face when Jason had made his comment told her how foolish she'd been.

She took a deep breath and took a big bite out of her ham sandwich. She didn't need Scott. She'd been alone all her life, and she could be again.

She'd vowed no one would hurt her again, but

it was too late now. She didn't know when she'd fallen in love with Scott, but it had happened. And as she'd feared, she had been rejected once more. Being alone was going to be harder than ever.

Scott sank down on the couch in the break room and tossed the bag containing his sandwich on the coffee table. He propped his elbows on his knees and buried his face in his hands. He couldn't believe what had just happened in the other room. Were his feelings for her so obvious that even a deputy who'd only been around him and Lisa a short time could see how he felt?

He should have said something, but he'd been so shocked he couldn't think. Lisa knew how his past still haunted him, but she couldn't understand how damaging to his emotional stability it had been.

It wouldn't be fair to ask any woman to share the life he lived. He didn't want her to see him when he woke up in the middle of the night shouting for medics to help his wounded and dying men. And he didn't want her to see him when the battle memories became so real that he paced the floor repeating the only words that could still his shaking body. She had no idea what he went through at times, and it was better if she never found out.

There was no use denying his feelings for her anymore. Everyone around him could see it, but he hoped she hadn't yet figured out that his attention to her was more than a police officer doing his job. He might joke that he aimed to please, but he was beginning to realize that he would love to spend the rest of his life doing just that for Lisa.

The ringtone of Lisa's cell phone drifted from the other room, and he sat up straight. Ever since she'd received those texts, he'd worried every time he heard her phone ring. He stood, walked to the door and waited for her to answer.

"Hello." She hesitated a moment, then spoke again. "Oh, hi, Travis. I've been meaning to call and thank you for stopping by to see me the other day."

Travis? Scott searched his mind for someone named Travis on the island. The only one he could think of was Travis Fleming. Scott had met him at church right after he came to Ocracoke, and his sisters really liked him. Satisfied the call was safe, Scott walked back to the couch and picked up his sandwich.

Ten minutes later, he walked back into the outer office. Lisa tossed the remains of her lunch in the trash can, but she didn't look up as he entered.

He stopped beside her desk and shoved his hands in his pockets. "Is Jason not back yet?"

"No. He checked in a few minutes ago. He was just leaving the beach. He should be here anytime now."

Scott nodded. "Good. I'll watch for him outside."

He waited for her to say something, but she began flipping through a stack of papers on her desk instead. He backed away. "Okay, I'll be back to drive you to Treasury's when Brock relieves me from duty."

"That won't be necessary."

He was halfway to the door when her words stopped him. He turned around and stared at her. "Why?"

She glanced up, and the chill in her eyes took him aback. "Travis Fleming called a few minutes ago. He asked me to go out with him tonight. He's going to pick me up here, and we're going over to Hatteras for dinner at the Barracuda Grill. He wants to try to make the five-thirty ferry, so I may be gone before you get off work."

His eyes grew wide. "You're going to dinner with Travis Fleming?"

"Yes."

"What time will you be back?"

She shrugged. "I don't know what else he has planned. The last ferry back is at midnight and the trip from Hatteras takes forty minutes, so it may be late. Why?"

He swallowed to relieve the parched feeling in his throat. "I thought I'd check to make sure you got home all right. After all, I don't know Travis well, and he is quite a bit older than you."

She glared at him. "Fifteen or sixteen years, but

what does that matter?" She stood up and crossed her arms. "Maybe you think you need to approve Betsy's dates and Emma's when she gets older, but I'm not your sister, Scott. I can choose my own friends. Do you have a problem with that?"

Scott shook his head. "No, not if that's what you want."

She tilted her head to one side and arched an eyebrow. "Who wouldn't want to go out with the most eligible bachelor on the island? He's wealthy and divorced and quite a catch for any woman. We've always been friends, and he's been concerned about me." She shot him a pointed look. "In fact, he came by here the other day to ask if he could do anything to help. He's always the first one to help out an islander when they have problems."

He felt like he'd been kicked in the stomach, but he couldn't let her know. "I've heard he's a nice guy. Have a good time, and I'll come by Treasury's to pick you up in the morning."

She directed her attention back to the papers on her desk. "Fine. See you then."

He whirled and hurried out the door. Jason pulled into the parking lot, and Scott charged toward him. Jason stepped out of the car. "Here you go, Scott. Thanks…"

Scott pushed around him and jumped in the vehicle before Jason could finish his sentence. He pulled into traffic and headed out to the beach.

When he arrived, he pulled into the parking lot and sat there with the motor idling. The air conditioner blew across his skin, but it couldn't stop the burning he felt.

He couldn't believe it. *Lisa has a date with another man.* He leaned forward and rested his head on the steering wheel. For days he'd tried to deny the feelings he had for Lisa because he knew they would only cause him grief.

Now he'd been proven right. He'd fallen in love with Lisa Wade, and the thought that she didn't return his feelings hurt worse than anything in his past.

TWELVE

Travis had kept up a steady conversation all through dinner, and Lisa was glad. She'd nodded her agreement from time to time and smiled at the right moments. Her reluctance to talk hadn't appeared to concern him, but then she suspected he was used to being in charge of every situation.

He paused midsentence and set his coffee cup in the saucer. He stared at it for a moment before he glanced up at her. "I'm sorry. I've rambled on and on without giving you a chance to talk. But I wanted this night to be special for you. That's why I brought you to Hatteras. I knew we wouldn't run into any of our friends who would want to grill you on how you've made it with all that's happened to you."

She smiled. "Don't apologize. I've enjoyed being here tonight. I've heard about the Barracuda Grill ever since it opened, but I'm afraid a dispatcher for the sheriff's office can't afford the prices here. Thank you for bringing me to such a swanky place."

His dark eyes stared at her from his suntanned face, and he smiled. "To tell you the truth I don't come here very much, either, but I've been thinking about you. When I stopped by the police station a few days ago, you looked so sad, and I couldn't get you off my mind. I wanted to do something to make you feel better." He cleared his throat. "The more I thought about it, I knew I needed to do something for myself, too. I work all the time and never go out. So, I guess this is my way of getting out for a good time and cheering up a friend in the process."

The sincere expression on his face lifted her spirits. "Thank you for wanting to help me."

He grinned. "You've helped me, too. Like I said...I don't get out much, but I've really enjoyed this meal. How about some dessert?"

She shook her head. "I don't think..."

He held up his hand to stop her. "I've heard the white chocolate cheesecake here is out of this world. Don't make me indulge myself alone. I won't feel as guilty if you eat some, too."

She laughed. "All right. I'll have some and a cup of coffee."

He motioned for the waitress. "Thanks, you've saved me from embarrassment."

Twenty minutes later, Lisa pushed her empty dessert plate away and drained the last drop of coffee. With a sigh, she settled back in her chair. "Thanks again, Travis, for a wonderful dinner. It's taken my mind off my problems being here."

"It's been my pleasure."

She leaned back in her chair and studied the handsome man across from her. "You have a reputation on Ocracoke for caring about your friends. I'm glad you consider me one of them."

He grinned. "And a mighty pretty one, I might add."

She could feel her face flushing, and she smiled. "That's quite a compliment coming from Ocracoke's most successful businessman."

He sighed. "Yeah, I've been fortunate in business, but not in my personal relationships. You know I'm divorced."

"Yes, I remember your wife. She was very beautiful."

"We were married right out of college, but she never could adapt to life on Ocracoke. I was busy learning to run our business, and I ignored her. She left and went back to the mainland."

"I'm sorry, Travis."

"She couldn't understand my way of life." He folded his napkin beside his plate and crossed his arms on the table. "When I was growing up, I knew my family was better off financially than my friends' families. But my father taught me that having money also gave you an obligation to help others who weren't as fortunate. I don't know how many islanders he helped through the years. My grandfather, I'm sorry to say, didn't share his beliefs, and they argued a lot about it."

"That must have been difficult for you."

"Yeah, it was," he admitted. "But since I've been the head of our family enterprises, I've tried to do what I thought would make my father proud. That's why I've thought about you so much. Is there anything you need? I'll be glad to give you the money if there is."

"I couldn't take your money."

He shrugged. "You could consider it a loan if it would make you feel better. I only want to help."

She reached across the table and squeezed his arm. "That's sweet of you to offer, but I'm fine. I still have my job, and Treasury Wilkes won't take any money for letting me stay at her bed-and-breakfast. My house may be gone, but I still have the property where it sat. As soon as the debris is cleared away, I'm going to have my real estate agent put it up for sale."

He looked down at her hand, and she pulled away. "I heard the reason you put the house up for sale was so you could leave the island. Do you still plan to go somewhere else?"

"Maybe. Right now I'm confused about what I really want."

He smiled. "Does that confusion have anything to do with the new Ocracoke deputy?"

Her eyes widened. "Scott? Why would you think that?"

He chuckled. "Everybody knows everything that happens on our island, Lisa. The grapevine has you and Scott Michaels practically married."

Her face flamed, and she sat up straight. "That's not true. Scott is a friend who's helped me with my problems."

"You mean like the break-ins and your house exploding?"

She couldn't meet his gaze. She glanced down and ran her finger around the rim of her coffee cup. "That and another problem that's popped up."

"Oh?"

"A family matter."

His forehead wrinkled, and he shook his head. "I'm sorry, Lisa. I didn't mean to pry."

"What you said about your wife not liking Ocracoke made me think of my mother. She hated life on the island, too."

He frowned. "I didn't think you would remember your mother. You were so young when she died."

"I don't remember her, but I've learned a lot about her lately."

"How?" The frown on his face disappeared, and his eyebrows arched. "Oh, the diary. I read about that in the newspaper."

She tapped her toe in exasperation. "Yes. I suppose everybody on the island knows about it."

He reached across and covered her hand with his. "I'm sorry about that. I told Terry Davidson he shouldn't have printed that article. It was an invasion of your privacy."

Tears pooled in her eyes. "Thank you."

He took a deep breath. "Enough talk about things that make us sad. I don't want to end the evening on a note like that. I'm going to be in meetings all day tomorrow, but I'd like to call you when I get through. I'd like for us to have dinner again."

A shaky smile pulled at her lips. Another date? She didn't know about that. She'd had a good time with Travis, but something hadn't seemed right about the evening. Even with their conversation and his sincere interest in her well-being, she kept wishing it was Scott sitting across from her. Yet after the way he'd acted at the station at lunchtime, she doubted if there would be any more evenings with him.

A few nights ago they had sat on the beach, and Scott had told her about God's love. It had made her believe there might be something better for her in the future, but today his attitude had told her it wasn't with him. There wasn't a future for her with anyone. The sooner she got off Ocracoke and jump-started her life somewhere else, the better off she'd be.

Scott leaned back in the front porch wicker chair and listened to the waves breaking on the beach behind the dune ridge next to the house. Still shaken from the nightmare that had awakened him, he concentrated on the night sounds around him. He wondered if he would ever be able to lie down and sleep without being alert for signs of something amiss. His nights would be more peaceful if he could rid himself of this holdover from his military service.

He relaxed in the quiet surrounding him. There was nothing to signal danger for his sisters sleeping inside the house. He smiled at the thought of Betsy and Emma, safe in their beds, and Kate who would soon be a mother at her home a few miles away. How did he ever get so lucky to be here with them?

To someone looking at his life from the outside, it might appear he had everything a guy could want—a family, a job he liked and a new start on a beautiful island. There was only one thing missing, and it was something he'd told himself over and over he could never have. A woman to share all the good things that had happened to him was what he truly wanted, but he didn't deserve it. And he sure didn't deserve someone like Lisa Wade.

Lisa's face flashed in his mind, and he winced. Where was she now? Still with Travis Fleming? The last ferry left Hatteras at midnight, she'd said. It was one-thirty in the morning, so she should be at Treasury's by now.

He glanced down at the cell phone in his hand. Several times he'd started to phone her but had changed his mind. She'd think he was out of his mind to call at this hour. And she would be right. If he was honest with himself, he'd admit he couldn't stand to think of her having a good time with another man. Not when all he wanted was for her to be with him.

The front door opened, and Betsy stepped onto the porch. "Scott, what are you doing out here?"

He sat up straight in the chair. "I couldn't sleep."

She eased into the chair next to him. "Was it another nightmare?"

He groaned and raked his hand through his hair. "Yes, but they don't come as often as they used to."

"You want to talk about it?"

He pushed to his feet and walked to the railing around the porch. His heart thudded. The dream tonight had been different. There were no wounded or dying men around him, just a road winding across a desert terrain.

He pressed his hands to either side of his head, but he couldn't erase the pictures forming in his mind. Why couldn't he talk about it? He'd kept it hidden for so long, even though he knew God was disappointed. He wanted Scott to tell the story to everyone he met. Others needed to know the message he had been given on that hot day. But he had failed God, just as he had failed so many others.

The memory he'd kept locked in his heart burst into his mind, and his head jerked back as if it had been rocked by an explosion. It had never seemed like the right time or the right person to hear it before, but now something had changed. God had given him the family he never thought he'd have. It was time to do what God wanted—tell the story he'd held on to for so long, and who better to start with than one of his sisters.

He took a deep breath. "When I went to the hospital in San Antonio, my doctors knew there was something I was hiding that could help me heal the emotional scars left by the war, but I wouldn't open up to them. God reminds me every day about it, but I've never been able to tell anyone."

Betsy leaned closer. "If it'll help you get better, you need to talk about it."

He closed his eyes and frowned, then rubbed his hand across his eyelids. "On my last assignment we were in very dangerous territory. It was impossible to tell our friends from our enemies. We had to be on alert at all times, but that didn't keep us from losing a lot of good men. I blamed myself for their deaths, for not protecting them. I'd come to the point that I took a lot of unnecessary risks by putting myself on the front line instead of them."

"I can see you doing that."

"The morning it happened, I had been awake all night thinking about the patrol we were going to do the next day. When we started out, I got in the driver's seat of the Humvee. The guy riding with me had just gotten word that his wife had given birth to a baby boy, and all I could think about was keeping him safe so he could get home to see his son. He was in a talkative mood that morning about the baby, but I couldn't listen for scanning the area for hostiles." He cleared his throat, then continued. "As the morning progressed and we didn't see anybody, I began to relax a little, thought maybe I'd worried about nothing. Then all of a sudden, a herd of sheep came out of nowhere. I hadn't seen them beside the road. They were just there all of a sudden and surrounded my Humvee. They filled up the road and walked in front so that I had to slow to a crawl."

She scooted closer to him. "What happened next?"

"The guy riding with me yelled at them to move and those behind us honked their horns for me to speed up, but I didn't want to run over the sheep. They just ambled along like they were out on a morning stroll and didn't scatter even with all the noise. Then all of a sudden there was an explosion that nearly threw me out of my seat. Dirt and rocks rained down on the top of our Humvee, and we ducked as best we could." He swallowed hard. "I thought at first we were under attack, but there wasn't a second explosion. The sheep ran off in all directions, and I climbed out of the Humvee. I couldn't believe what I saw. I had to grab the side of the vehicle to keep from collapsing."

"What did you see?"

"Just feet in front of my Humvee was a crater in the middle of the road where an IED had exploded. I walked to the edge of the hole and looked down. Then my knees did buckle, and I dropped to the ground. A dead lamb lay in the bottom of the crater. That lamb had led the way when the sheep crowded in front of me, and he ended up giving his life for me."

"Oh, Scott," Betsy gasped, "you could have been killed."

He nodded. "But I wasn't. The lamb had sacrificed its life for me. I knelt on the side of that big hole and stared down at the lamb, and I knew God had sent me a message that day."

Her forehead wrinkled. "What kind of message?"

"When I went into the military, I felt alone and didn't think there was anybody who loved me." He grasped Betsy's hand. "I didn't know about you and Kate and Emma. I thought I was destined to be by myself forever, but God told me that day I wasn't alone. He reminded me someone else loved me and died for me long before that lamb did on that desert road. Jesus, the Lamb of God, came to be a sacrifice for my sins." His voice grew thick with emotion. "God spoke to me and told me if I really believed that, He could help me through anything. He would always be with me. I do believe that, Betsy. But why don't I act like I do?"

Betsy chuckled. "Our faith is weak sometimes, but it sounds like you know where to turn when yours is."

"I do. Every time something happens to remind me how fragile life is, I say 'Remember the lamb.' I say it over and over, and it's like God wraps His arms around me to protect me."

"God watched over you that day."

"And many more after that." He smiled at her. "Like He did the day I came to meet my family. God's been telling me He'll take my wartime memories away, but I haven't let Him have complete control over my healing. I think I can do that now."

"You just have to put your complete faith in Him."

"You're the first person I've ever told that story to, but you can't be the last. God knew He was going to bring me to you, Kate and Emma, and that really started me on the road back. Now I've got to start giving His message to other people who are hurting. If I do that, I think I can put the past behind me."

Betsy didn't say anything for a moment, then she leaned over and kissed Scott on the cheek. "I'm glad I was the first person you told. I love you, Scott. Like Emma says—you're the best big brother any girl could have. We've noticed the changes in you since you came to the island. God has a way of working miracles here on Ocracoke."

"Yeah, He does." In the distance a black-crowned night heron called out, and Scott closed his eyes. God was everywhere here, and he wanted Lisa to know that, too. "I need some sisterly advice with another problem."

Betsy stared up at him. "What is it?"

"I don't know what to do, Betsy. I've told myself over and over there's no place for a woman in my life until I face my problems. Then Lisa comes along, and I can't think straight."

Betsy reached up and caressed his cheek. "Scott, you are a wonderful man, and you deserve to have somebody to love. You said God knew He was going to bring you to us. Lisa may have been part of that big plan, too. Don't limit God. Let Him give you all the wonderful things He has planned for you."

He shook his head. "I want to do that, but I think I've put an end to anything happening between Lisa and me."

"What do you mean?"

He took a deep breath and related the events that had taken place in the office at lunchtime. "And now she hates me, and she's out on a date with another man."

Betsy buried her face in his shoulder and chuckled. "Oh, Scott. Lisa doesn't hate you. Jason's words may have frightened her as much as they did you. Then after you wouldn't eat with her, she decided she'd have to show you that you weren't the only guy interested in her."

His mouth gaped open, and he stared into her eyes. "You think so?"

"I do. After all, she has her pride. A girl can't let a guy think she's going to be available whenever he has time for her. We like to keep the men in our lives guessing what we're going to do next."

"If that's what she's trying to do, she's succeeding."

Betsy grinned. "Well, good for her. The two of you have spent so much time together lately, you may have started thinking Lisa is going to be there waiting for you to tell her what to do next. No girl likes to be taken for granted. This may be her way of letting you know you'd better make up your mind about your feelings before she looks somewhere else."

He shook his head. "I think my problem is that I don't understand women."

"And that's the way we women like it." She hugged him and laughed. "Especially with you strong silent types who have a hard time telling a girl how you feel. Just remember this, Scott—if God hadn't spared your life on that desert road, you never would have met Lisa. He may have had her in the big plan for your life even before you knew her."

"Do you really think so?"

"I do, but you're the one who needs to believe it, too." She stifled a yawn. "Now, I'm going back to bed, and I suggest you get some sleep, too. You have work to do tomorrow, and some of it is called mending fences."

He kissed her on the forehead and watched as she disappeared back into the house. Once again he breathed a prayer of thanks to God for bringing him to his sisters. They had been better medicine for him than anything his doctors had prescribed in the past.

He leaned against the railing and stared up at the twinkling stars that always reminded him of God's presence. Betsy's words about how God might have brought Lisa into his life to make it better rang in his ears. He wasn't sure about that. Not yet. But a small hope that she might be right burned in his heart. Now if he could figure out how to apologize to Lisa for his behavior today, she might give him a chance to find out if Betsy was right.

THIRTEEN

The makeup Lisa had put on this morning couldn't hide the dark circles under her eyes. She leaned closer to the mirror and studied her reflection. Her sleepless night had left its mark on her features. With a sigh, she picked up the brush from the dresser and pulled it through her hair.

She must have watched the minutes click off on the digital clock by her bedside all night long. All she could think about was Scott's abrupt attitude with her yesterday at the station. It seemed his personality had changed without warning. One minute he acted happy and caring, and the next he'd shifted into what she'd begun to call his shutdown mode. When that Scott appeared, she had no idea what to expect. If that was any indication of what a relationship with him would be like, she needed to rethink the possibility of anything developing between the two of them. She didn't want to end up like her mother——looking for love from someone else because her husband didn't have time for her.

She grabbed the tube of lipstick on the dresser and swiped it across her lips, then stepped back to review her appearance. Satisfied that she'd done all she could to make herself presentable, she reached for her handbag at the moment a knock sounded at the door.

Frowning, she strode across the room and threw the door open. Her heart pounded at the sight of Scott standing in the hallway. As always, his uniform clung to his body and enhanced the muscles in his arms and chest. Happiness at seeing him bubbled up in her before she recalled the events of the day before.

She flipped her hair over her shoulder and propped her hand on her hip. "What are you doing here?"

Her skin burned from the searing gaze that raked her face. "I drive you to work every morning. Remember?"

So he wasn't here to see her. He had only come out of a sense of duty because he'd promised to drive her back and forth to work. Disappointment pricked her heart. She whirled to pick up her purse. "I'll just be a moment."

When she turned around, he'd stepped into the room. "Did you have a good time last night?"

She looped the purse strap over her shoulder and

lifted her chin. "I did. Travis took me to a fancy restaurant, and I enjoyed the evening."

"That's good."

She studied the man before her, a handsome sheriff's deputy who could make any woman's heart race, but there was another side to him—one she feared. The Scott who still relived the memories of the battlefield frightened her, but her own past haunted her even more. The choices she'd made had chiseled a chunk out of her soul, and she didn't know if she could ever really trust a man again.

"I've known Travis all my life, and he thought I needed to get out and have a good time. He was right. I'm sure you have better things to do than spend all your time keeping tabs on me, and I need to be with other people."

He blinked. "Is that what you want?"

She took a deep breath. "Yes, but I hope we can still be friends."

His eyes narrowed, and he nodded. "I'll always be your friend, Lisa. But there's something I need to tell you." He rubbed the back of his neck. "About yesterday. I want to apologize about my behavior at lunch. I had a lot on my mind."

"There's no need for that. I understand how stressful your job can be. I was concerned, though. You slammed the door so hard when you left I was afraid you had broken the hinges."

He looked away. "Yeah, I guess I acted like a jerk. I won't do that again."

She eased across the floor and stopped in front of him. He was so close she could smell his aftershave. She longed to put her arms around his neck and pull his lips down to hers. Instead she stepped back. "You're not a jerk, Scott Michaels, but you need to be honest. I think your reaction yesterday might have been brought on because you don't want me to find out if Ean Thornton is my father."

His jaw tensed, and he stared at her. "I know we can't help who our parents are, but I really hope Ean isn't your father. You're a good friend, and I only want to save you from heartache."

Disappointment flowed through her. She'd hoped he would take her in his arms and tell her he would help her find out for sure, but he hadn't. He'd called her a good friend. There was no need to fool herself any longer. Scott Michaels was just like everybody else in her life. He didn't want her, either.

After a moment, she cleared her throat. "I think it's time we left for work, but first let me get my mother's journal. I want to go back over some of the entries and see if I can figure out her connection to the *Elena*." She turned back to the dresser and opened the drawer where she had placed the diary. She gasped and whirled to face Scott. "It's gone."

He strode toward her. "What do you mean?"

"The diary. I put it in this drawer yesterday morning, and now it's not here."

He looked down at the open drawer. "Are you sure this is where you put it?"

"Yes, I always keep it here. I put it in there before I left for work, but I didn't get home until late last night. I didn't check it then."

Scott shook his head. "This doesn't make sense. Why would anybody take it?"

"I don't know, but it could have been anytime yesterday." Tears gushed from her eyes. "Oh, Scott, my mother's diary. What am I going to do? That's all I had of her."

He turned and hurried toward the door. "Let's ask Treasury if she saw any suspicious people here yesterday."

Treasury looked up from kneading a mound of dough when they walked in the kitchen. Lisa rushed to her. "Treasury, someone's been in my room."

The elderly woman pulled her hands from the dough and picked up a towel. "Is there anything missing?"

"My mother's diary. It was in the dresser drawer, and now it's gone."

Treasury wiped her hands and shook her head. "I sure hope I don't have a guest that's a thief. Was there anything else missing?"

Scott shook his head. "Not as far as we know.

But I want you to think back to yesterday. Did you see anyone who acted suspicious around the house, maybe somebody out of place like they didn't belong here."

Treasury's forehead wrinkled in thought, but after a moment she shook her head. "No, not that I recall. Just the usual delivery people and my guests."

Lisa covered her face with her hands. "This doesn't make any sense."

"Think again, Treasury," Scott said. "Are you sure you didn't see anybody else?"

"No, just Lisa's cousin Jeff."

Lisa jerked her head up and stared in astonishment at Treasury. "Jeff? Where did you see him?"

"He was in the upstairs hallway. I had just come out of cleaning one of the guest rooms, and I spotted him. He said he had stopped by to see you, but you weren't here. I thought it was kinda strange that he didn't know you'd be at work at that time of morning. He thanked me and left."

Scott leaned closer. "Did you see him come out of Lisa's room?"

Treasury shook her head. "No, but come to think of it, I did hear a door close before I stepped into the hall."

Scott turned to Lisa. "Didn't you lock your bedroom door before you left yesterday morning?"

"I did. How could he have gotten in?" She had

no sooner uttered the words than the answer came to her. "Jeff's father was the island locksmith, and Jeff still has all his tools."

"Maybe that explains how the intruder got in your locked house," Scott said.

Lisa's heart thudded. "You don't think Jeff could have been the person who did all the damage to my house and then killed Wayne instead of me?"

Scott pursed his lips. "It's possible." His cell phone rang, and he glanced at the caller ID. "This is Brock. I'll tell him we need to pick Jeff up for questioning right away." He put the phone to his ear. "Brock, I was just about to call you." Scott's face suddenly paled. "Where?"

Lisa inched closer to Scott. "What is it?"

He held up a hand to silence her and listened for a few more moments. "I'm at Treasury's now picking up Lisa. We'll be right there."

Lisa grabbed his arm as he ended the call. "What's happened?"

"That was Brock. He's out at the beach. Some tourists found a body there this morning—and he wants us to come down."

Lisa frowned. "Why me?"

Scott took a deep breath. "Because the dead man is Jeff. He's been shot."

Lisa pressed her hand to her mouth and sank into a kitchen chair. Treasury hovered over her. "Lisa, darling, are you all right?"

Concern for her lined Treasury's wrinkled face. Kate, Betsy and even Scott had often referred to her as their second mother, and Lisa could understand why. Treasury cared deeply for everyone around her, and she never failed to offer comfort where needed. At this moment Lisa needed someone to lean on, and she was glad Treasury was there.

She put her arm around Treasury's waist and hugged her. "I'll be fine. I just can't believe Jeff is dead. In spite of all his problems, he was still family."

Treasury nodded. "Of course he was."

Lisa sighed and pushed to her feet. "I suppose I'd better go with Scott now. I'll see you when I get back."

"My patrol car's out front," Scott said. "Let's go."

Lisa trudged through the house and onto the front porch. A group of laughing teenagers rode down the street on bicycles, and in the distance she could see gulls circling over Silver Lake Harbor. It looked like any other day on Ocracoke, but it wasn't. Jeff, her last relative, was dead, but her real father was out there somewhere. An overwhelming desire to find him filled her.

Scott nudged her in the back, and she started down the steps. Earlier Scott had said he wanted to be her friend, but he hadn't made any promises about a relationship. He had, however, once promised he would help her find her father. She hoped he would follow through on what he said. At the moment she needed to put her sorrow at Jeff's death and her feelings for Scott aside. It was time to concentrate on discovering her father's identity.

A small crowd hovered near the road when Scott stopped the patrol car at the beach entrance. Lisa was out of the car almost as soon as it stopped. Brock and two EMTs stood near the edge of the water looking down at Doc Hunter, who knelt beside the still form of a man on the sand. Scott caught up with Lisa when she was about halfway to Brock.

He grabbed her arm. "Lisa, don't go any closer. Wait here."

She bit down on her lip and nodded. "Okay."

Scott eased forward and stopped beside Brock. "I brought Lisa. She's waiting back there. What do you have so far?"

"Nothing much. Some tourists out for an early-morning walk found him. He has several gunshot wounds. Until Doc tells me differently, I assume that was the cause of death. Doc says the body will have to go to the state lab in Raleigh for an autopsy, and you know how backed up they are. It may be weeks before we get any results on whether or not they found DNA or anything else we can use in the case." He glanced back at Lisa. "I'm glad I caught you while you were still with Lisa. As the only living relative, she'll have to identify the body."

"Before you talk to her, there's something else you should know."

Brock listened as Scott related what had happened at the bed-and-breakfast. When he had finished, Brock gave a low whistle. "So you think Jeff may have been the one who's caused Lisa's problems?"

"It makes sense."

Brock nodded. "Yeah, it does." He glanced back to the body on the beach. "But this presents us with another problem."

The same thought had repeated in his head all the way to the beach. "Yeah. Maybe Jeff wasn't the one who wanted Lisa out of the way. Whoever killed Jeff could have his own reasons for making sure he didn't talk."

Brock pushed his sunglasses up on his nose. "And the only thing he could do was silence Jeff forever."

Brock and Scott stared at the body again, and Brock nodded. "That sure makes sense, all right. The only problem is I have no idea how we're going to prove it." He glanced over his shoulder at Lisa. "Let's go talk with her."

Lisa didn't move as they approached her. Her

gaze flitted from Scott to Brock. "Scott said Jeff is dead."

Brock nodded. "He is. I'm sorry, Lisa."

She exhaled. "I am, too. He was such a happy boy growing up. His life changed a lot when he started doing drugs in high school. I really thought we had a good relationship, but Scott thinks he might be the one who broke into my house."

"That's right," Brock said. "I have some news to share with you. Yesterday I received the latest phone records for your cell and home phones. The last call to your house was from the same cell phone that sent the first texts, but the last text was from a different number."

"This doesn't make sense." She frowned and shook her head. "Jeff was on the ferry on his way to the mainland when my house exploded."

Scott glanced at Brock. "It sounds like the perfect alibi, doesn't it? But the fire chief still thinks a spark from that ringing phone set off the explosion. Jeff could very well have made the call from the ferry. As for the other text, maybe someone closer made the second one."

Lisa's body trembled, and she wrapped her arms around her waist. "I can't believe Jeff would hate me so much to do this."

Brock put his hand on her arm. "At this point it's only conjecture. We'll search his house, though. If we find anything to support our suspicions, I'll let you know."

She smiled. "Thanks, Brock. If there's anything I can do to help, let me know."

He bit his lip. "I hate to ask this, but I need you to give us a positive identification of Jeff. You can do it here or at the health center."

She took a deep breath. "I'll do it here."

Brock led Lisa to the body, but Scott hung behind and scanned the crowd that had grown in the last few minutes. Grady Teach appeared to have a captive audience for spewing the latest tale he would soon be spreading throughout the village. When Lisa, looking a little green around the gills, stepped back beside him, Scott grasped her hand. "Are you all right?"

She bit her lip and nodded. "I'm okay."

He stared at her a moment before he turned to Brock. "Do you need me for anything else? Or is it all right for me to take Lisa back to the station?"

"I'll finish up here and meet you back there." Brock turned and headed back to Doc Hunter, who had risen to his feet.

Scott grasped Lisa's arm and pulled her toward the police cruiser. She didn't speak as he drove back through the village. When he stopped in the police station parking lot, she swiveled in the seat, dried her tears and faced him. "I've been thinking

about Jeff all the way back, and I think I understand why he may have been willing to hurt me."

"Why?"

"When our grandmother left me the house, I
could tell he was angry, but I thought he'd gotten
over it. After all, she had paid out more on his drug
treatment programs than the house is worth. So he
really got more from her than I did."

"A lot of good it did him," Scott sneered.

"I thought it had, but maybe he was still using
and needed money. Do you think he thought with
me out of the way the property would pass to
him?"

Scott shrugged. "I don't know, Lisa. He could
have wanted money, and somebody was willing to
pay him to do those things."

She raised a brow. "What are you talking about?"

He wanted to take her hand in his. Instead he
gripped the steering wheel tighter. "Somebody
killed Jeff. Right now we don't know why. It could
be a drug deal gone bad, but it could have been
something worse. It's possible somebody didn't
want him to tell what he knew about all your problems."

She shook her head. "I can't believe that. Why
would anybody hire Jeff to hurt me?"

"I don't know. Maybe we've looked at this case
all wrong. When you surprised the intruder in your
house, he could have killed you while you were

unconscious, but he didn't. Then when he trashed your house, it was more like he was angry at you instead of wanting to hurt you. It wasn't until later that the text messages began and your house blew up."

Lisa frowned. "But what does that all mean?" Her forehead wrinkled as if she were in deep thought, and then her eyes grew wide. A small gasp escaped her mouth. "Those things happened after the article about me finding the journal appeared in the paper," she whispered.

Scott nodded. "That's right. Maybe somebody on this island doesn't want what's in the journal made public." He pointed to the police station. "Let's go inside and wait for Brock. We need to discuss this together."

They climbed from the car and headed toward the building. With each step Scott glanced over his shoulder. At this point his belief about the reasons behind Jeff Wade's death was just a theory, and he had no idea how to find out the truth.

He glanced at Lisa. Her eyes streaked red from crying sent a protective surge of emotion spiraling through him. He had promised her he wouldn't let anything happen to her, and he intended to keep that promise. Now it appeared finding Jeff's killer might be the only way he had to keep his word.

FOURTEEN

Lisa had no idea how many times she had glanced at the clock since she and Scott had arrived at the police station. It had been hours since they'd left the beach, but Brock still hadn't arrived. With Deputy Lewis out on patrol, Scott had roamed the office all morning like a caged animal and had barely spoken two words to her.

She clenched her teeth and stared at the computer screen. She felt like jumping out of her skin waiting for Brock to update them on the investigation.

Ten interminable minutes later, the front door opened, and he finally walked in. She winced at the tired look in his bloodshot eyes. He set the police equipment bag he held on Lisa's desk and dropped into a chair beside her. He rubbed his hand across his face and glanced up as Scott came out of the break room. "Glad you're here, Scott. I want to run some things by you."

Lisa jumped up from her chair. "Let me get you a cup of coffee. You look like you need one."

He shook his head. "I'm okay. I've been up all night on duty and have it again tonight. As soon as I catch you two up on what's happened, I'm going home to bed."

Lisa sank back into her chair. "Did you search Jeff's house?"

Brock nodded. "Yeah. And we found this."

He opened the equipment bag and pulled out a polyethylene evidence bag. Lisa gasped at the sight of her grandmother's ring inside. "Where did you find it?"

"In a dresser at Jeff's house. This was beside it." He pulled out another bag that contained a cell phone. "We dialed the number of the phone that sent the first texts to you, and it rang."

"What about my mother's journal?" Lisa asked.

Brock shook his head. "Sorry. We didn't find that, but we'll search again."

"What could he have done with it?" She hit the desk with her fist. "I can't believe I was so naive. Jeff came to the health center the day after my attack and acted concerned. And all the time he was the one who had hit me over the head and taken my grandmother's ring. I wonder why he didn't pawn it."

Scott leaned closer to get a look at the ring. "He probably was waiting until he thought it would be safe to get rid of it."

"But there's something I don't understand," she said. "I received a threatening text while we were still at my house after the explosion. If Jeff was on the ferry, how did he know I hadn't died?"

Brock shrugged and pushed to his feet. "I don't know yet, but we're going to find out. It reinforces our theory of another person being involved. If we're right and he killed Jeff, you may be in more danger than ever. We've got to keep a closer watch on you than ever before."

Lisa glanced at Scott, but his face didn't reveal how he felt about Brock's suggestion. "I appreciate that, but you can't protect me forever."

Scott frowned. "But we want to, Lisa."

She shook her head. "No. You and Brock have all you can do without adding me to your list." She turned to Brock. "I've already taken up too much of Scott's time. Deputy Lewis is here in the daytime, and I'll stay close to Treasury's house in the evenings until you've solved Jeff's murder."

Brock glanced at Scott and back to her. "There's a problem with that scenario, Lisa. I talked to Sheriff Baxter this morning, and Jason is being called back to the mainland. It's just going to be Scott and me for now until he can send someone else."

"Even more reason for me not to be a bother to you."

"Lisa, I've told you from the beginning we're just doing our job," Scott said. "All we want to do is protect you."

The curt tone of his voice shocked her. He couldn't have made his feelings any plainer. She was the victim of a crime, and the time he'd spent with her had been out of a sense of duty.

Before she could respond, Brock spoke up. "Let's not argue about this. Both of you are right. We're shorthanded at the moment, and Lisa needs protection. I think I have the solution."

"What?" Scott asked.

"I recently read about an app for your cell phone that can be used for tracking your friends. It's easy to download, but your friends have to agree to being tracked. I think the three of us need to download the app and sign up on the website to track each other." He glanced at Scott. "That way, we'll know where Lisa is even when we're not with her."

Scott tilted his head and stared at her. "Are you all right with us knowing where you are all the time?"

"Of course I am."

He raised his eyebrows. "I wouldn't want you to think we were spying on you, especially if you were out on a date."

Brock glanced from one to the other. "Date? Have I missed something?"

"I believe you were the one, Deputy Michaels, who said we were friends. I'm glad to have friends who would go to such lengths for my protection." She pulled her cell phone from her purse. "Tell me how to download this app to my phone, Brock."

Within minutes they'd downloaded the app to each phone and added each other as friends. Brock slipped his phone in his pocket and closed the equipment bag. "I wish I could give the ring to you, Lisa, but it's evidence right now. Maybe it won't be too long before you have it back."

"That's all right. Now, you go get some rest."

Brock ran his hand across the five-o'clock shadow on his face and grinned. "Yeah, but I'll be back later."

Scott shook his head. "Don't be in a hurry. Let me stay later tonight to give you more time at home."

"Are you sure?"

"Yes. Enjoy spending some time with your wife."

Brock slapped Scott on the shoulder. "Thanks, buddy. I'll see you later."

Lisa crossed her arms and looked at Scott when the door closed behind Brock. "Why don't you go get some lunch before Jason gets back?"

He glanced at his watch. "I think I will. Now that I can track you I feel better about leaving you alone. I'll be back in about thirty minutes."

She dropped in her chair and directed her attention back to the computer. When the door closed behind him, she looked up and leaned back in her chair. Scott might have been beside her all morning, but he'd seemed like he was in a different world. His usual attentiveness was gone, and in its place there was a cold aloofness.

A tear rolled down her cheek at the thought they wouldn't share any more moments like the one on the beach the night of Treasury's birthday. Scott had assumed his shutdown mode, and she didn't know how to bring back the man she'd come to love.

Scott clenched his fists and marched down the street to the Sandwich Shop. He had no idea what had happened between Lisa and him this morning. His main reason for going to her room earlier had been to apologize for his reaction to her assumption that Ean Thornton might be her father, but he had also wanted to tell her about the talk he and Betsy had the night before. Then everything had changed.

From the time she opened the door, he could see she was in a bad mood and could care less about anything he could tell her. She seemed to enjoy throwing her date in his face and then telling him they'd been seeing too much of each other. Instead of mending fences as Betsy had suggested, the encounter with Lisa had widened the gulf between them.

When he'd told her about Jeff's death, he'd thought for a moment she might turn to him for comfort. Instead it was Treasury who'd offered solace. Later at the beach he could tell she was upset when she identified Jeff's body, but she'd still kept her distance from him. It wasn't hard to figure out the message she'd sent. She had no interest in seeing where their relationship might go.

Then when Brock had suggested the app for the phone, he'd almost been glad. At least he had a valid excuse for not being with her. He could still track her whereabouts, but he wasn't sure he wanted to do that. He didn't want to know if she was out with Travis Fleming. Angry at himself for his conflicting feelings, he stomped up the steps to the deck outside the Sandwich Shop.

It wasn't until he'd ordered that he remembered he hadn't asked her if she wanted anything. He pulled his cell phone from his pocket but hesitated before he punched in her number. With a groan he slipped the phone back in his pocket. No need to call her. He didn't want to hear the icy tone of her voice again. It hurt too much.

Lisa tried to concentrate on the traffic tickets Scott and Brock had given out over the past few days, but it was no use. She might as well have been a hundred miles away instead of staring into an open filing cabinet. Her mind kept returning to the question she'd asked herself after the conversation with Grady. Could Ean Thornton really be her father?

She had to admit that Scott's warnings contained some truth. She'd known Mr. Thornton all her life and had never liked him. His son Mike had terrorized motorists on the island in the fast cars his doting father had bought him and had been kicked out of some of the best schools in the state. Mike's belief that he was untouchable had imploded when Kate had arrested him for murder.

Lisa pressed her hands to her face at the thought of her friends Kate and Betsy. What would they think if Ean turned out to be her father? Would they turn their backs on her or be happy for her finding out the truth? She didn't have to ask about Scott. He seemed to already have made his decision.

She slammed the door of the filing cabinet shut and shook her head. It didn't matter what anyone thought. She had to find the answer.

The front door opened, and she glanced around at Jason entering the office. "Sorry, I'm late. Is Scott here?"

"No, he's at lunch."

He grinned and dropped a sack on the desk he'd used for the past few days. "I picked up something for myself. Why don't you go eat? I'll cover for you until Scott gets back."

She started to say she wasn't hungry, but an idea popped into her head. The residents of the island knew each other well and were aware of each other's habits. All the successful businessmen ate lunch every day at the Red Snapper down the street. If she went there to get something to eat, she just might run into Ean Thornton.

"Thanks. I appreciate that." Lisa grabbed her purse and headed for the door. "I won't be gone long."

He held up his sandwich. "They have a special over at The Coffee Cup. Where are you going?"

"I think I'll go to the Red Snapper. I haven't eaten there in a while."

Jason frowned. "But that place is so busy at lunch, you may not be able to get a table."

"Then I'll wait." She patted her purse. "I have my cell phone if you or Scott need to reach me."

She rushed out the door and down the sidewalk. She needed to get out of there before Scott returned. He would be upset if he guessed the real reason she wanted to go to the Red Snapper. Grady had given her the first clue that might lead her to the identity of her father, and she needed to pursue it.

She had no idea what she would do if Ean Thornton really was there. You couldn't just walk up to a man in a public place and ask him if he was your father. There had to be some way she could approach him. Nothing came to mind. If he was there and she had a chance to speak to him, she'd have to wing it.

Customers jammed the dining room of the Red Snapper when she entered. Clutching several menus in her hand, the hostess hurried toward her. "Hi, Lisa. You haven't been here in a while. It's good to see you."

Lisa smiled at the petite brunette who'd been in her class at the island school. "Hi, Amber. I'm usually so busy around lunchtime I grab a bite at my desk, but today I thought I needed a treat. This was the first place I thought of."

Amber beamed her approval and glanced over Lisa's shoulder. "Anybody joining you?"

"No. Table for one."

Amber frowned and scanned the dining room. "The only thing I have is near the kitchen. Is that okay?"

Lisa glanced at the table across the room. It sat in the perfect spot for her to observe everything around her. "That's fine."

Moments later, Lisa lowered the menu and stared over the top. There were some tourists in the establishment, but most of the people eating today were friends or acquaintances. She didn't see Ean Thornton among them.

As the minutes ticked by, the crowd began to thin out. Lunchtime appeared to be ending for the island businessmen. As she chewed the last bites of her salad, disappointment roiled in her stomach. Her idea of running into Ean Thornton hadn't materialized. Or maybe he'd come and gone before she arrived.

With a sigh, she picked up the check her waitress had left and opened her purse. Laughter caught her attention, and she glanced up to see Amber leading Ean to a table a few feet away from her. And he was alone. She tried to still her beating heart, but it was no use.

He dropped into his chair, pulled on a pair of reading glasses and began to study the menu. She searched his features to see if she saw any resemblance to her own, but she didn't. Taking a deep breath, she summoned her courage and rose from her chair.

As she approached his table, she slowed until she came to a stop beside him. "Mr. Thornton, how are you today?"

A surprised look flashed on his face, and he glanced up. "I'm okay." He leaned back in his chair. "I was sorry to hear about your house and about your cousin's death. You've had a lot of problems lately."

She nodded. "Yes, I have. I wondered if you might have time to talk to me a minute."

He glanced at his watch. "I'm in a hurry today. I told Amber I needed fast service."

Her throat ached, and she swallowed to relieve the parched feeling. "I don't want to detain you, but I need to speak with you. It's about my mother."

He cleared his throat. "Roxanne?" He hesitated

a moment before he sighed and motioned her to sit. "How can I help you?"

She settled in the seat and clasped her hands in her lap. "I've been told you were friends with my mother. In fact, you were one of her best friends at the Sailors' Catch Pub where she used to go."

He leaned forward, laced his fingers together on the tabletop and frowned. "What are you getting at, Lisa?"

"I want to know more about my mother. I have reason to believe you were very close to her."

He furrowed his forehead. "Oh, I get it now. I read in the paper about the journal. You've been reading it, and you want to find out all her secrets. Well, you've come to the wrong person." His voice turned to steel. "That was a long time ago. Before I was married, in fact. I liked your mother, but she was a married woman. We were friends. I enjoyed spending time with her. End of story."

Lisa struggled to hold back the tears. "But there has to be more."

"There isn't anything more," he growled. "I've answered your question. Now you need to go."

"I was told you had feelings for her. Maybe she had some for you, too. Can't you tell me if that's true?"

His face turned red. "That was nearly thirty

years ago. What difference does it make what happened back then?"

"It makes a difference because I have to know if you're my father." Unable to believe what she'd just said, she clamped her hand over her mouth and cringed.

Ean's fist struck the table with such force she thought it might collapse. "How dare you come in here, interrupt my lunch and make such an accusation," he snarled. "It wouldn't surprise me if your good friends Kate and Brock Gentry put you up to this. They'd do anything to cause me trouble."

The wild anger in his eyes terrified her, and she shrank back in her chair. "No, please believe me. They had nothing to do with this."

He leaned forward and gritted his teeth. "Now, you pay attention to what I'm about to say. I want you to stay as far away from me as you can. If you ever come near me again, you'll be sorry. Have I made myself clear?"

"Y-yes."

He glanced at the check in her hand and jerked it free. "Tell you what, I'll pay for your lunch today. It's compliments of a man who thought a lot of your mother. Too bad her daughter didn't inherit some of her good sense."

Lisa jumped up from the table and ran from the restaurant. Tears streamed down her face. She didn't know where she was going. All she wanted was to get away from the anger in Ean Thornton's face.

She stopped about halfway between the restaurant and the police station and sat down on a bench in front of a souvenir shop to catch her breath. Noisy tourists filled the sidewalks and drifted in and out of the shops. She watched the families on vacation and brushed away the tears on her cheeks.

A chime from her cell phone signaled an arriving text message. It was probably Scott wondering why she was late to work. With a groan, she pulled the phone from her purse and opened the message. A gasp tore from her throat, and she jammed her fist in her mouth at the words she read. *I have the journal, and I know your secret. You'd better keep your mouth shut, or you'll wind up like your mother.*

Terrified, she jumped to her feet. This message couldn't be from Jeff. Could it be from Ean Thornton? Or was there someone else she didn't know about?

Brock and Scott had been right. Somebody besides Jeff wanted to harm her, and now it looked as though he would stop at nothing to keep her from finding out the truth about her mother's death.

Without knowing where she was headed, she ran across the street, around the corner and onto the next street. She ran until her legs threatened to collapse. When she stopped, she realized she was in front of the church she'd attended on Sunday with Scott and his sisters. Panting for breath, she eased up the steps and pushed on the front door. To her surprise it opened.

Light filtered through the windows and spread a peaceful glow across the quiet surroundings. She sank into a pew at the back, crossed her arms on the bench in front of her and bent her head to rest on top of them.

Her breathing slowed, and her body relaxed. It was as if someone sat beside her and wrapped arms of love around her. Was this what Scott had talked about? Could she be experiencing God's love?

She straightened and stared at the cross hanging on the wall behind the pulpit. The words she'd read in Treasury's Bible trickled through her mind like bubbling water in a stream. She closed her eyes and lifted her face toward heaven. Her blood warmed her veins, and she basked in the glow of an unseen presence.

"Jesus, are You here?" As if in answer, her heartbeat quickened, and her stomach fluttered. She knew she wasn't alone. "Jesus," she whispered. "I believe. Help me."

In that moment, she knew her life had changed forever. A soothing peace flowed through her and with it came an assurance she would never be alone again. She might never know her father, and Scott might never return the love she felt for him. But that wasn't as important as it had seemed earlier. Now God walked with her, and she would never be alone again.

"Lisa." Scott's voice surprised her, and she jumped at the sound. He stood in the aisle and stared at her. "What are you doing here?"

She smiled and rose to her feet. "Getting things straight in my life." She wiped her eyes. "How did you know where I was?"

He held up his cell phone. "I tracked you. I was worried because you hadn't gotten back to the office."

She glanced at the cross again and then turned to him. "Thank you for bringing me here Sunday. Now I feel like I can face anything that's thrown at me because I know God is with me."

His eyes raked her face. "I'm glad to hear that. You want to tell me about it?"

She took a deep breath. "Not now. We need to go to work. I'll tell you all about it later."

But she knew she wouldn't tell him about the text message. He would be frightened for her and would insist on staying close, as before. She didn't want him to protect her out of a sense of duty. When and if he wanted a relationship with her, he had to want it because he loved her as much as she did him.

She only hoped it would happen before she came face-to-face with a killer who knew the answers to the mystery in her mother's journal.

FIFTEEN

Lisa dreaded going home from work this evening. Usually she had left work by now. Not tonight. She'd stayed because she wanted to talk to Scott about her experience at the church this afternoon. He had pulled extra duty to give Brock some more time at home and had gotten tied up with the near-drowning of a teenager at the beach. With him still at the health center and Jason's departure on the last ferry, she was all alone in the station.

She glanced at her watch again and wondered if Treasury had saved her any supper. It was nearly seven o'clock, and she had started to get hungry. There was no telling how long Scott would be at the health center. She could talk to him in the morning.

As she did every night, she forwarded the incoming local calls to Brock's cell phone and notified the mainland terminal she was leaving. They would relay all emergency calls from the island to the appropriate responders. She scribbled a quick note to Scott telling him she'd gone home and would see him in the morning.

She'd just finished writing the note when her cell phone rang.

"Hello."

"Lisa, it's Travis. I've been in closed-door meetings all day and just heard about Jeff. How are you holding up?"

She took a deep breath. "I'm okay, but it's been a rough day. How did you find out?"

"I ran over to the Sandwich Shop to get something to eat, and Grady was in there telling everybody about it."

"I should have known the answer before I asked."

Travis hesitated a moment. "That wasn't all he said."

The pulse in her neck throbbed. "What else did he say?"

"He, uh, he said one of the waitresses at the Red Snapper said you had a confrontation in there with Ean Thornton today. He said you accused Ean of being your father. Is that true?"

She closed her eyes and bit down on her bottom lip. "Oh, no," she moaned, "I can't believe someone heard that."

"Then it's true? I wanted to tell you because I thought Grady had made it up."

She shook her head. "No, it's true. It's probably all over the island by now."

"But I thought…" His voice drifted off, then he cleared his throat. "It doesn't make any difference what I thought. Do you need someone to talk to? I can try to help you figure out what to do about this."

Tears filled her eyes. "Oh, Travis, thank you. I do need a friend."

"Then I'm available. I'm still at my office. Have you eaten yet?"

"No. I haven't left the station."

"Then why don't you meet me here?" he suggested. "We can grab something to eat later."

"That sounds good. I'll be there in ten minutes."

"Good. I'll see you then."

Lisa grabbed her purse, threw her cell phone inside and ran to the door. She had to get out of here before Scott came back. If he had already heard about the incident at lunch, he would probably be furious with her. He'd warned her about approaching Ean, and she hadn't listened. Now it looked as though she was going to pay dearly for her poor judgment.

On the sidewalk she broke into a jog and headed toward the offices of Fleming Enterprises. She only hoped Travis could think of something that might stop the rumors from flying. If not, there was only one thing to do—leave the island. That's what she'd intended before this nightmare began, and now she'd have to follow through. But things had changed in the past few weeks. She'd fallen in love with Scott and couldn't stand the thought of leaving him.

It couldn't be helped. The secrets from her past couldn't be allowed to hurt Scott and his family. She would do everything she could to make sure that didn't happen.

Scott exhaled and climbed from the police cruiser. It had been a long day, and he was glad to be back at the police station. The incident with the near-drowning had turned out all right, but it had been touch-and-go for a while. Now all he wanted was to get home, eat some dinner and go to bed. He hoped Brock had arrived to take over. Then he could take Lisa to Treasury's house and get home.

When he entered the station, he looked around in surprise. Where was Lisa? After looking in the break room, he walked back to her desk and spied her message. Gone home? Why hadn't she waited, as he'd told her to do?

Irritated at her disregard for his concern, he pulled his cell phone out and dialed her number.

"Hello."

He frowned at the panting in her voice. "Lisa? I came back, and you were gone. Are you okay?"

"I'm fine. I just had to leave."

Her answer didn't make sense. "But why? Is something wrong?"

"I told you I'm fine. Let's just leave it at that." The sharp tone of her voice felt like a jab in his stomach.

"Are you home yet?"

"No, but I will be later."

"Then where…" He stopped and sank down in the chair at her desk. There was only one reason she would be so evasive with him. She had to be with someone else. "Are you with Travis?" He closed his eyes and hoped her answer would ease his pain.

"Yes."

He took a deep breath. "I see. Well, I just wanted to make sure you're all right. Have a good night."

He disconnected the call before she had time to reply and slipped the phone in his pocket. Regret that he hadn't told Lisa how he felt washed over him, but he shook the thoughts from his head. It wouldn't have done any good. He could never compete with a man as rich and handsome as Travis Fleming.

"Hey, Scott, what's the matter? You look like you're in outer space."

Scott glanced up at Brock, who had entered the station. Scott rubbed the back of his neck and pushed to his feet. "I'm tired. That's all."

For the next few minutes, he caught Brock up on all the calls he'd answered today. When he'd finished, Brock glanced around. "Where's Lisa? I thought you'd drive her back to Treasury's."

Scott took a deep breath. "No. She had other plans tonight. I talked to her, though, and she said she'd be home later."

Brock's eyes narrowed. "Other plans? How do you feel about that?"

Scott shrugged. "Not much I can do about it. I think I blew my chance with Lisa."

"I'm sorry, Scott."

"Yeah, me, too," he said wearily. "Now I'm going home. Call me if you need me."

"Will do."

Scott stopped outside the police station and stared up at the stars. Not too long ago he and Lisa had looked at the stars together and talked about how beautiful they were on Ocracoke. He had thought God might be opening a new door in his life, and he hoped Lisa would be the prize behind the door. Now it didn't look like that was ever going to happen.

He squinted at the stars that dotted the heavens. "God, I love her so much, and I do want her to be happy. Watch over her for me."

His assurance that God had heard his prayer comforted him, but he couldn't get Lisa out of his mind. Something wasn't right, but he had no idea what it might be. All he could do was to wait for God to show him.

* * *

Lisa had never been in Travis Fleming's office before. She'd driven by the building for years and had never given a thought to what went on inside. The Fleming family had roots on the island that went back to the early twentieth century, and over the years their business ventures had flourished and expanded to faraway places on the mainland as well as overseas.

The picture of a woman and a young boy sat on Travis's large mahogany desk, and she picked it up. "That's my mother and me." She glanced up at Travis, who had reentered the room carrying a tray with two cups on it. "There was still some coffee in the pot, and I poured us some when I left those papers on my secretary's desk."

Lisa smiled and set the framed picture back in its spot. "Your mother was very beautiful. Where is she now?"

He handed her a cup, took one for himself and sat down in the chair next to her. "She lives down in Florida on a beachfront estate I bought for her. She loves the water."

She took a sip of the coffee. "You sound like a good son."

He stared at his mother's picture for a moment before he responded. "I try to be. She had a tough time living with my father. When I was about ten, she decided to leave the island, but my grandfa-

ther and father wouldn't let her take me with her.
I visited her on holidays and in the summers." A
shadow crossed his face. "When I'd leave, she'd cry
and tell me how sorry she was she hadn't stayed
with me, but she'd been driven away by my father
and grandfather."

"How awful for her and for you."

"Yeah. All they were interested in was an heir to
the fortune my grandfather had amassed, and they
were through with her after my birth. I promised
her that when I was in control of everything, I'd
take care of her...and I have."

"I'm sure she's very proud of you."

He took a long drink of his coffee. "Is your coffee all right?"

"It's fine." Lisa lifted the cup to her lips and
swallowed.

Travis leaned back in his chair and crossed his
legs. "Now tell me what made you approach Ean
Thornton today. I thought your father was killed
in a boating accident."

"So does everybody else." For the next few minutes she told Travis about the discovery that another man was her father, her suspicions about the
Elena, and her thoughts that perhaps her mother
was murdered.

When she finished, he stared at her, amazed.
"This is incredible. So you think your real father

might still be alive and that he might have some link to the sinking of a ship years ago."

She drained her coffee cup and set it back on the tray. "I know it sounds wild, but that's what I believe. And I wanted to find out the truth."

"Do you still want to do that?" he asked.

She thought for a moment before she answered. "Before I came over here, I was ready to give up and leave the island. But you've been so kind and understanding, it makes me believe that other people might be, also. Maybe I need to stay here and find out who my father is. Then I can put some closure to this whole nightmare."

He set his cup next to hers and shook his head. "But you may not like what you find out."

"I know. Scott has warned me of that. In fact, he'd be furious if he knew I talked to Ean today." She sighed. "But with Grady spreading the news, he'll probably find out sooner or later."

"I suspect he will. And you're okay with that?"

"I can't say I'm okay with everybody knowing, but it's hard to hide the truth. If it's going to come out, I might as well face up to it."

Travis scooted to the edge of his chair and propped his hands on his knees. "This is a big decision, Lisa. Are you sure you want to find out the answers?"

"I do."

He tilted his head and narrowed his eyes. "No matter what it costs you?"

"Yes."

"Then I'll help you." Travis glanced at her cup. "More coffee?"

She shook her head. "No, thanks. Are we going to dinner? I'm hungry."

He stood and held out his hand. "I think it's time we left."

She grasped his hand and pushed to her feet. Her legs wobbled, and she braced her free hand against his chest. "I feel a little dizzy."

He eased her back into her chair. "Why don't you sit down a minute? It's probably because you haven't eaten."

She blinked her heavy eyelids and tried to focus on him. There appeared to be two of him standing in front of her and wavering back and forth. She rubbed her hand across her eyes. "I have the strangest feeling…"

He walked back behind his desk and sat down, then folded his hands on top and leaned forward. "Rest a minute until you feel better. In the meantime I'll tell you a story."

She frowned. "What kind of story?"

He arched an eyebrow. "About a man who made a fortune being a rumrunner in the early part of the twentieth century."

She yawned and shook her head. "What man?"

"My grandfather was just a kid himself, but when Prohibition came along, he saw an opportunity to make some money. He scraped together every penny he could to buy a boat, and he ended up making a fortune smuggling liquor up the East Coast." He paused for a moment. "Then he got the idea of branching out a little more. He and his crew started to board the ships they came across and rob them. The *Elena* just happened to be one of them."

She tried to sit up straighter, but her body wouldn't respond. "Your grandfather robbed the *Elena?*"

Travis chuckled. "Yeah, and after that he and his crew had a lot of money. So they stopped their rumrunning, and he settled on Ocracoke. It was remote enough that he could begin a legitimate business. He bought his first boat and started his commercial fishing business. Before long he had a fleet." His tone filled with admiration. "That man was the shrewdest businessman I've ever known, and he taught me everything he knew. The only regret of his life was that his son didn't take after him. My father hated the business, and he didn't love my mother. He only married her to give my grandfather an heir and was glad when she left. For my sake, though, he hung in there until I was grown and could take over the business. That's what my grandfather wanted, too."

Lisa laid her head against the back of her chair

and closed her eyes. "I don't understand. Why are you telling me this?"

"Because I want you to know about my family. Anyway, I went away to college, and I thought things were fine. That is, until I found out my father had been having an affair with the wife of one of our employees and had fathered a child. He had told my grandfather that he was going to leave the island and take the woman, who was by then a widow, and his three-year-old daughter somewhere else to live." His voice hardened. "The worst part was that he had given his mistress my grandfather's mirror from the *Elena,* and she was threatening to tell the story unless my grandfather agreed for them to leave."

Lisa's eyes flew open, and she leaned forward. "Y-you're talking about me and my mother."

He nodded. "I am. You see, Lisa, I've always known about you and your mother."

She tried to smile, but her lips wouldn't cooperate. "Then that means…"

"That's right. We're brother and sister."

"But, Travis, why have you never told me?"

He shrugged. "Because I didn't want anyone to know our business was started by illegally gained money, and I thought the secret was safe. My grandfather and your mother are both dead, and my father has Alzheimer's. Then I read the newspaper about you finding your mother's diary. I suspected what you'd found out." He opened a drawer in his desk and reached inside. "I had to know what was in it."

Her breath froze in her throat, and chills raced up her arm. He held her mother's journal. "H-how did you get that?" she stammered.

"Jeff gave it to me. Right before I shot him."

Her eyelids drooped, and she forced them open. "You shot Jeff?"

A laugh rattled in his throat. "Are you having trouble focusing? It could be from what I put in your coffee to help you relax."

She wanted to rise, but she doubted if she could stand. "I don't understand."

He sighed, shoved the diary back in his desk and came around to stand in front of her. "Then let me explain. When I heard you were going to leave the island, I thought I'd hurry you along. Jeff was still angry over not being in your grandmother's will, so I hired him to scare you, to hurry your exit from the island." He exhaled sharply. "Then when I read the paper, I knew we had to take drastic measures. If you had stepped in your house that day, it could have all been over. Jeff couldn't wait to find out if you were dead. He had to call, and from what I hear that's what set off the explosion."

Lisa rubbed her forehead and tried to concentrate. "But I didn't die."

Travis sighed. "I was at the Sandwich Shop when

Grady came running in telling everybody about Wayne Simms. I had a cell phone that couldn't be traced, and I sent you a message. Did you get it?"

Her head lolled against the back of the chair. "That was you?"

"Yeah. Too bad about Wayne, but I sent flowers to his memorial." He paused for a moment. "Anyway, after Jeff stole the diary, he read it before he gave it to me and decided he wanted more money. He shouldn't have done that."

Even as sleepy as she was, she could hear the evil in his voice. Something clicked in her drugged mind. "You," she whispered. "You're the evil one my mother wrote about."

He leaned against the front of his desk and crossed his arms. "Is that what she called me? If I am, it's her fault. I came home from college one weekend and found out Dad was determined to leave with the two of you, and he wanted you named in my grandfather's will." He leaned closer. "No way was I going to share my inheritance with you. I took the lighthouse key my dad had and sent a note to your mother telling her to meet me there. I signed my father's name."

Lisa shook her head. "No, don't tell me anymore."

"But that's not the end. I left the door unlocked like he always did. She was shocked when she got to the widow's walk and found me instead of my father. She put up quite a fight, but in the end I threw her over the side."

Tears streamed down Lisa's face. "You're evil just like my mother said."

He straightened to his full height. "I call it determined. My father almost went out of his mind with grief, but my grandfather was glad. He convinced my father they had to protect me. He never had been able to take a stand against my grandfather, and in the end he agreed. He told me later she didn't even have the mirror. She had mailed it back to the ship's owner."

Lisa's chest heaved with sobs. "Why did he protect you?"

"Because I'm his son."

"And I'm his daughter." She tried to push to her feet but sank back in the chair.

He stared down at her. "I don't think he ever forgave himself for deserting you. He never missed an opportunity to see you when you were growing up. He attended all your school plays and sporting events. He never did that for me."

"H-he did?"

"Yeah, and one day, before I took him to the nursing facility, his mind was clear. He made me promise I would tell you he really loved you." He chuckled. "So now I've told you, and you're the only one left who knows the truth."

Lisa rubbed her forehead and tried to think. "No,

there's someone else, the park ranger who gave your father the key. Surely he suspected something."

Travis shrugged and chuckled. "I don't know. He died soon after your mother's death. His boat exploded while he was fishing. The islanders could hardly believe two tragedies could happen so close together."

"I'm going to tell Scott and Brock. You won't get away with this." She gritted her teeth and pushed to her feet, but her legs collapsed. Travis caught her before she fell.

He held her upright and reached for her purse. He looped the strap over his shoulder and hoisted her into his arms. "I don't think you're going to tell anybody."

Her eyes blurred, but she tried to focus on Travis's face. "What are you going to do?"

"Don't worry, little sister. It'll be over soon. It's too bad you're so distraught over everything that's happened. I'm sure the villagers will think it caused you to jump from the lighthouse widow's walk like your mother did. What a tragedy."

She tried to lift her hand to scratch at his face, but her arms hung limply next to her now-relaxed body. A dizziness overwhelmed her, and she fought the sleep that was overtaking her. The more she fought, the faster she drifted toward unconsciousness.

Her head rested against Travis's chest, and she

could feel the beating of his heart. Her last conscious thought was of Scott and how she would never see him again.

SIXTEEN

Lisa's eyes blinked open, and she frowned. Her head pounded, and she lifted rubbery arms to press her temples. Nausea roiled in her stomach, and she tried to focus her vision.

"Are you awake?"

The question startled her and she glanced at Travis, who sat next to her. She tried to straighten but couldn't. A tight seat belt held her in place. She turned her head to stare out the window of the car as it jerked to a halt. Fear turned her blood cold. Travis had pulled to a stop down the street from the island lighthouse.

She reached for the door handle, but he caught her arm. "We're going to have to sneak past the lighthouse keeper's house, and you have to be quiet. This ought to do it."

Unable to fight him, she closed her eyes and waited as he tied a gag around her mouth. He climbed from the car and pulled her out after him. She tried to raise a fist to strike at him, but couldn't. Her body swayed back and forth in front of him. She had to get away, find help.

She turned to run, but only took two steps before her legs gave way, and she stumbled to her knees. Travis knelt beside her. "It's no use."

The muzzle of a gun rubbed up the side of her face. "Try that again, and I'll finish you right here. Do you understand?"

She nodded.

He pulled her to her feet, forced her back toward the car, and pulled her purse from inside. He hung the bag from her shoulder, stuck the gun in her back and whispered in her ear. "Now, don't make a sound when we pass the keeper's house."

He pushed her onto the walkway that led to the entrance to the lighthouse. She glanced up at the structure that had withstood the hurricanes on Ocracoke since 1823. Its light beamed against the darkness from seventy-five feet up. High above, the widow's walk circled the area around the lens room. She thought of her mother and wondered what she had felt facing Travis that night twenty-five years ago at that height. A tear ran down her face.

Travis nudged her along the path through the darkness, past the keeper's house and the small building where maintenance supplies were housed, and to the entrance of the lighthouse. He positioned her between his body and the door and pulled a set of keys from his pocket. He held them up and laughed. "Compliments of Jeff. I think they'll find these as well as this gun next to your body. One more tragedy to add to your mental state. You must have taken his keys after you killed him."

The door swung open, and Lisa's legs collapsed once more. Her purse slipped from her shoulder and hit the ground. He grabbed her around the waist and forced her inside. Lisa glanced over her shoulder at her purse outside the door as he closed them inside the entrance.

She blinked in the darkened entry. Her eyes slowly focused, and she spied a metal staircase winding up toward the top of the lighthouse. Travis jerked the gag from her mouth and stuffed the cloth in his pocket. "You can scream all you want now. These walls are five feet thick, and no one's going to hear you." He glanced up at the staircase. "We have quite a climb. I know you aren't up to it, but I'll help you." He grabbed her arm and stuck the gun in her back. "Now, let's go."

"Travis, you don't have to do this. I don't want any of your money."

"That's what you say now, but you'd change your mind," he sneered.

"No, I won't. Please think about what you're doing. I'm your sister."

He leaned forward until they were face-to-face. "That's why I have to do this. Now, move."

Lisa swallowed back her fear and turned around. Before she could take a step, she thought of the time she'd spent in the church earlier. She had left there knowing whatever happened she wasn't alone. Now that knowledge filled her with peace. Whatever happened, she wasn't climbing toward the widow's walk alone.

She looked up at the stairs that wound upward, and dizziness overcame her. There was no way she could do this on her own. She needed strength from somewhere else.

I need You, God. Help me.

Scott tried to concentrate on the movie Emma had picked out for them to watch, but it was no use. He couldn't shake the restless feeling he'd had ever since arriving home. Beside him Emma laughed out loud. Betsy stuck a kernel of popcorn in her mouth and smiled at their little sister, who had seen this film at least five times.

Betsy pushed to her feet and headed toward the kitchen. "The coffee should be ready. Want a cup, Scott?"

"Yes, please."

He watched his sister leave and glanced back at Emma, who appeared oblivious to his presence. "Tell Betsy I'm on the porch, will you?"

Emma frowned at him. "You're leaving? This is the best part."

He sighed. "I know. I thought so the first three times I saw it. I'll be outside."

Without waiting for an answer, he strode through the front door and onto the porch. He walked to the railing and leaned against it. What was the matter with him? He raked his hand through his hair and took a deep breath. Something wasn't right, but he didn't know what it was.

The front door opened and Betsy, holding two cups of coffee, stepped onto the porch. "Emma said you were out here. What's the matter? You couldn't listen to those chipmunks sing another minute?"

He laughed and reached for the cup she held out to him. "I'm restless. I don't know what's caused it, but I can't sit still. It's the same kind of feeling I used to get when I knew there was a dangerous mission coming up."

Betsy frowned. "That's strange. Did anything happen at work today that might have triggered this?"

He shook his head. "Nothing I can think of. Maybe I'm just tired."

She sat down in one of the wicker chairs and took a sip from her cup. "You haven't told me how things worked out with you and Lisa. Did she accept your apology?"

"I guess so."

Betsy sat up straight, the movement jarring her cup. "What do you mean by that?"

He shook his head. "It's complicated. She's not interested in me after all. It seems Travis Fleming has become her good friend. In fact, they're out together tonight."

Betsy's eyebrows arched, and she rose to her feet. "Oh, so that's why you're restless. You're jealous."

His face warmed, and he took another sip of coffee to give him time to think of a reply. "No. I want her to be happy. It's just…I don't see her with Travis Fleming. He's so much older than she is."

Betsy laughed. "I think that sounds like you're jealous. Where did they go?"

"I don't know. I started to check my GPS, but I don't want her to think I'm checking up on her when she's out on a date."

"GPS? I don't understand."

"It was Brock's idea." She listened as he told her about the app they had downloaded on their cell phones earlier today. "It's to make sure she's safe."

Betsy inched closer, a mischievous grin on her face. "Don't you need to know if she's safe now?"

He pulled his cell phone from his pocket and stared at it for a moment before he shook his head. "No, I can't do that."

Betsy's eyes softened. "You're a very special person, Scott. Most men would be so eaten up with jealousy they'd track her every step."

"Yeah, well, most men don't have a lot of unanswered questions about whether or not they even deserve to have a relationship with a woman."

Betsy shook her head. "You've got to stop thinking like that."

Before he could respond, his cell phone chimed, and he glanced down at the caller ID before he connected the call. "Hi, Brock, what's up?"

"I'm tied up with a head-on collision between the village and the Hatteras ferry. I'll probably be here for some time. But I was wondering if you had talked with Lisa."

"No. Why?"

"I checked the GPS on my cell phone just now, and it seemed strange. I thought she might be with you."

"No. Where was she?"

"It showed her position at the island lighthouse. Kate has told me how Lisa never goes there, but that's where it shows she is."

"The island lighthouse? Are you sure?" Scott gripped the railing of the porch.

"That's what it says."

A tremor went through Scott's body, and he whirled to face Betsy. "Something's wrong, Brock. Lisa would never go there. Never. She told me she drives out of her way to keep from going by there."

"I think we'd better check this out," Brock said. "I can't leave here. Can you go see what's going on?"

Scott rushed into the house and ran toward his bedroom. "I'm on my way."

"Call me when you know anything."

"Will do."

He disconnected the call, grabbed his holster and buckled it around his waist. He turned to see a shocked Betsy in the doorway. "What's the matter, Scott?"

"I don't know. I'm afraid Lisa's in trouble. If something happens to her, I'll never forgive myself."

He ran from the house and within moments was speeding toward the island lighthouse. The clock on the dash clicked off the minutes as he urged the car to move faster. He should have listened to his gut feeling that something wasn't right and checked on Lisa's whereabouts.

When he turned the corner to the lighthouse, he frowned at the sight of a car parked by the roadside. He'd seen Travis Fleming driving an SUV like it. For a second his belief that Lisa was in trouble wavered. He would feel foolish if he found Lisa and Travis out for a moonlight stroll around the base of the lighthouse.

He shook his head. Lisa wouldn't go for a walk at the place where her mother died. He skidded to a stop in the lighthouse parking lot and was out of the car almost before it came to a stop. As he ran toward the tower, he scanned the area but saw no one. The only sound he heard was a dog barking a few streets over.

Something on the ground at the front door of the lighthouse caught his attention, and he came to a stop. He stooped down, picked up Lisa's purse and looked inside. Her cell phone stuck out of a side pouch. His muscles tensed as they had every time he'd entered battle, and he knew he was right. Lisa was in trouble and needed help.

He pulled his gun from the holster and pushed on the door. A creaking noise echoed through the interior as the door swung open. With both hands on the gun, he stepped into the entrance and scanned the small area that housed a metal staircase that wound upward.

"Lisa, it's Scott!" His voice bounced off the walls. "Where are you?" A noise from above like a footstep on metal caught his attention, and he eased onto the steps. "Lisa! Can you hear me?"

"Scott, up here." The muffled voice from above turned his blood cold.

Ready to fire his weapon, Scott charged up the steps. As he ascended the second curve of the darkened steps, he spotted them. He could make out the form of Travis Fleming leering down at him from the steps above. He held Lisa in front of him with a gun pointed at her head.

"That's far enough, Deputy. Come any closer, and I'll kill her."

Scott halted but didn't lower his gun. "Let her go, Fleming."

A laugh rang out from where they stood. "If you want her, you're going to have to come and get her."

"Scott," Lisa cried out, "be careful. He'll kill you. He's already killed so many, one more won't make a difference."

"That's right, Deputy. You'd better listen to her. Throw down your gun and come on up."

Scott hesitated, unsure of what to do. He wouldn't give up his gun to save his own life, but Lisa's life was different. Should he drop the gun on the chance he could save her? He knew the answer. Without his gun they would both be dead.

A cry rang out from above, and he saw movement. He squinted in the darkness and realized Lisa was striking at Travis's face. Scott bolted upward and was only a few steps away when Travis cracked his gun across Lisa's face, aimed the barrel at Scott and fired.

"Scott!"

He heard Lisa's scream of agony at the same time the bullet pierced his body. He grabbed for the railing but couldn't catch hold. With a groan he tumbled backward down the steps until he landed on the concrete floor at the bottom. He lay there panting for breath.

Travis Fleming's voice cut through the silence. "Your boyfriend can't help you now. Get up those steps."

Muffled sobs drifted down the staircase.

Pain radiated through Scott's body. His hand brushed the front of his shirt, which was sticky with his own blood. He could feel it trickling down his side and knew with every heartbeat his life was pumping out onto the lighthouse floor.

He had to get to Lisa. The memory of how he'd tried to get to the wounded in battle and failed replayed in his mind. This couldn't end like that. He couldn't fail her as he had so many others.

The picture of a lamb, dead from a roadside bomb, flashed in his mind. That lamb had given his life to save him. Jesus had given His life, too, not only for him but for Lisa. Now it was time for him to offer his life as a sacrifice for the woman he loved.

Praying for strength, he pushed up on his knees and felt around in the darkness for his gun. His fingers touched the barrel, and he scooped up the weapon. Pain ripped his body, but he struggled to his feet and headed for the stairs. He groaned as he mounted the first step.

He clenched his jaw against the excruciating pressure in his side with each step and began the long climb. He could see no one on the stairs as he ascended, and he pushed his body onward. The stairs ended at a metal ladder that led through an opening into the lens room. He shoved his gun in the holster and gripped the bottom rung with the arm opposite his wound.

Biting down on his lip to keep from screaming out, he hauled himself up the ladder rung by rung until he emerged at the base of the lens. He shaded his eyes from the bright light and stumbled toward the door leading to the widow's walk.

"No, Travis, don't do this." Lisa's voice sent a new surge of energy through him.

He drew his gun and tottered onto the small walkway around the top of the lighthouse. To his left he spotted Lisa struggling with Travis. He had his arms around her waist and was trying to lift her, but she had her legs braced against the railing and her fingers clamped around the top bar. Travis's gun wasn't in his hand.

"Fleming! Get away from her!"

Travis let go and whirled to face Scott. Surprise mingled with hatred on his face. "I thought I'd killed you."

"Not quite." Scott cocked the gun. "Now get away from her before I forget I'm a police officer." Travis looked back at Lisa before he released her. Scott motioned toward the wall of the lighthouse with his gun. "Now raise your hands and get over there away from her."

Travis raised his hands and backed toward the wall. Keeping his gun leveled at Travis, Scott stumbled toward Lisa until he stood between her and Travis. "Are you all right?"

"Yes," she whispered. "Oh, Scott, he killed my mother and Jeff, and I thought you were dead."

"I'm okay. Are you sure he didn't hurt you?"

"He gave me a sedative, but I think it's wearing off. My cheek hurts where he hit me with his gun. I was so scared until you showed up."

Scott turned his attention back to Travis. "Where's your gun?"

Travis nodded with his head toward where Lisa stood. "I laid it over there."

Scott glanced over his shoulder to the spot Travis indicated. "Where?"

"Scott! Look out!" Lisa screamed.

He jerked his head around just in time to see Travis pulling a gun from the belt at his back. Instinct kicked in, and Scott fired. The impact knocked Travis backward through the door into the lens room. The gun clattered to the floor and Travis gripped at his stomach. He turned and took one step before he sprawled facedown on the floor.

Scott stumbled forward and grabbed the gun that lay beside Travis before his legs gave way, and he sank to the floor next to him. Lisa ran in from the widow's walk and dropped to her knees beside him.

Tears streamed down her face. "Are you all right?"

He groaned. "Get my cell phone out and call 911. Tell them we have an officer and murder suspect both down. We need medical help right away."

Lisa pulled the phone from his pocket, and he heard her making the call. He had to fight to stay conscious until help arrived. He couldn't leave her unprotected until someone got here.

"Scott, help is on the way. Stay with me until they get here."

He licked his lips and frowned. "I'll try."

She grasped his hand and kissed it. He could feel the tears dripping on his fingers. "Don't you dare die on me, Scott Michaels. I love you too much to let you leave me. Hang in there a few more minutes."

His heart skipped a beat, and he gazed up at her. He hoped he wasn't dreaming. She'd just uttered words he'd longed to hear. Her hand still grasped his, and he squeezed it. "That's good. Because I love you, too."

The wail of sirens drifted on the night air. They grew louder the closer they came to the lighthouse. Within minutes footsteps pounded on the stairs, and emergency responders burst into the room. Arnold Tucker, the EMT who'd been at Lisa's house the day it exploded, dropped to his knees beside Scott.

"Scott, can you hear me?"

Scott groaned. "Hi, Arnold. I'm hanging in there. What about the other guy?"

Arnold opened his medical bag and pulled out a stethoscope. "Don't worry about him. My partner's taking care of him."

Scott tried to push up to get a look at Fleming, but he sank back to the floor. "He's a suspected murderer. When you get him to the health center, I want him cuffed to the bed."

Arnold stuck the ends of the stethoscope in his ears and wrapped a blood pressure cuff around Scott's arm. "You got it, buddy. Now relax and let me take care of you. Doc Hunter is waiting for us at the health center."

Scott stared up into the face of the man who'd answered many calls with him since he'd come to Ocracoke. Arnold had become a friend like so many others on the island. When Scott had arrived on the ferry a year ago, he'd had no idea how his life was about to change. Now he had friends, a family and a woman who'd said she loved him. God had brought him a long way since the day a lamb had saved his life, and he would spend the rest of his days thanking Him for all the blessings he'd received.

His gaze drifted past Arnold, and he saw Lisa

talking on his cell phone. Her eyes met his, and she mouthed the same words she'd said to him minutes ago. He breathed a prayer of thanks that God had watched over them tonight.

Scott relaxed as he hovered on the brink of unconsciousness. He tried to spot Lisa again, but his eyelids drooped. He could rest now. She was safe. He smiled and closed his eyes.

SEVENTEEN

Lisa paced the waiting room floor of the health center. Scott was unconscious when they'd arrived in the ambulance, and she hadn't seen him since they had taken him into one of the exam rooms. She wanted to be with him, but Doc Hunter had given her strict orders to stay put until he called her back.

The front door flew open. Kate, Betsy and Emma charged into the room. Tears ran down Kate's face. "Where is he?"

"Doc Hunter's with him. He won't let anybody come back there."

Betsy strode toward the door that closed off the hallway where the exam rooms were. "I want to see him."

Lisa grabbed her arm. "Doc said he'd come out as soon as he knew anything."

Emma burst into tears. "Is Scott going to die?"

Betsy hurried back to her little sister, wrapped her arms around her and led her to the couch. She sat down and gathered the child closer to her. "He's not going to die, Emma."

Betsy's eyes pleaded with Lisa to reassure her. Lisa blinked back her tears and smiled at Emma. "We have to believe he's going to be all right, Emma."

The door banged open, and Brock charged into the room. He rushed to Kate, who began sobbing again and collapsed against him. Brock held his shaking wife in his arms. "What happened?"

Lisa took a deep breath. "Why don't we sit down, and I'll tell you."

When she had finished her story, she dissolved into tears. "I'm so sorry. I should have listened to Scott and been more careful about looking for my father. It almost cost me my life, and Scott may die."

Emma bolted up from the couch, her fists clenched at her side. "I thought you said Scott wasn't going to die."

Betsy pulled her down beside her. "We need to pray for Scott. Can you sit here and do that?" Emma nodded and buried her face in Betsy's lap.

The door from the hallway to the exam rooms opened, and Doc Hunter walked into the waiting area. They were all on their feet before he'd taken two steps. Doc pushed his glasses up on his nose and slipped his hands into the pockets of the white lab coat he wore.

Lisa tried to speak, but her vocal cords felt frozen. Kate grasped Brock's hand and stared at the doctor. "How is he?"

A somber expression covered Doc Hunter's face. "That's one tough brother you've got. He's made it fine so far, but we need to get him to a hospital. We're going to transport him by helicopter. I've already notified the hospital, and they'll be ready to take him to surgery when he arrives."

"When is he leaving?" Betsy asked.

"The helicopter is on its way. It should be here in a few minutes."

Lisa stepped forward. "May we see him before he leaves?"

Doc Hunter chuckled. "I don't want to risk the wrath of four women plus the chief deputy on Ocracoke, so I'll let you see him for just a minute."

Brock cleared his throat. "We've been so concerned about Scott, I haven't asked about Travis. How is he?"

"We're airlifting him, too. So if you have official business with him, you'd better do it now."

Brock nodded and turned to Kate. "I'll check on Travis and then be in to see Scott."

Lisa followed Scott's sisters, who hurried down the hallway behind Doc Hunter. When they came to a room at the end of the hallway, he opened the door and stepped back for them to enter. Kate rushed to one side of Scott's bed, and Betsy and

Emma to the other. Lisa entered the room and stood at the foot of the bed.

Scott's face appeared paler than it had before they'd left the lighthouse. She gripped the foot railing of the bed and pursed her lips. It was her fault he was hurt. *Please, God, let him live. I'll do anything to make it up to him for nearly getting him killed.*

Kate bent over Scott and smoothed his hair back on his forehead. "Scott, can you hear me?"

He opened his eyes and stared up at her, then turned toward Betsy and Emma. "Hey, Emma. How did the chipmunk movie turn out?"

Emma burst into tears again. "I—I d-didn't finish watching it. W-we'll watch it together when you come home."

He tried to smile, but his lips trembled. "You've got a deal." He blinked and frowned. "Where's Lisa?"

"I'm right here, Scott." She stepped from the foot of the bed to stand beside Kate.

He took a deep breath and lifted his hand. She wrapped both her hands around his. "Have you told them yet?" he asked.

Kate frowned. "Don't exert yourself, Scott. Lisa told us everything that happened."

Lisa smiled down at him. "I haven't told them the most important thing that happened at the lighthouse."

Betsy glanced from one to the other. "Then tell us."

Scott's gaze drifted over his sisters and came

back to rest on her. "I think I fell in love with Lisa the day I walked into the Ocracoke Island Sheriff's Office and saw her sitting at her desk. It's taken me a while to come to the point that I could believe I'm really worthy of her. But I love her with all my heart, and she says she loves me, too."

A stunned silence filled the room. Lisa glanced at each of Scott's sisters. Shock and disbelief lined their faces. Tears filled Lisa's eyes. "I love Scott more than I can tell you, and I want to spend the rest of my life making it up to him for almost getting him killed."

Scott moved his head sideways on the pillow. "You can't blame yourself for what happened with Travis tonight. But I have to admit I like what you said about spending the rest of your life with me." He looked at Emma and winked. "I believe we've got us another recruit for the chipmunk fan club."

Emma's eyes grew wide. "Really?"

Scott tried to raise his head. Pain flickered on his face, and he fell back against the pillow with a groan.

Lisa bent over him. "Don't try to talk now. Wait until later."

A wobbly smile pulled at his mouth. "I have something to say now. Kate, Betsy and Emma, I want you all to witness this moment." He squeezed Lisa's hand. "Lisa Wade, I love you so very much. Will you marry me?"

Lisa bent over until their noses almost touched. "Scott Michaels, it would be an honor."

She leaned forward, and their lips touched in a kiss that sent her heart soaring.

When she pulled away, he smiled. "I've wanted to do that for a long time."

"We've got a lifetime to catch up," she whispered.

Applause rippled through the room, and she straightened. Kate put her arm around Lisa and hugged her. "Oh, Lisa. You've been my best friend for so long that I feel like we're already sisters. Now it's going to be official."

Doc Hunter stepped into the room and stopped at the foot of the bed. "What's the clapping about?"

"I just got engaged," Scott said.

Doc chuckled. "Good, but the wedding is going to have to wait until we get you taken care of. The helicopter's here. We're transporting you and Travis on the same one. Say your goodbyes so we can load you."

Lisa clasped Scott's hand tighter. "Can I go with him?"

Doc frowned, and Lisa waited for him to tell her no. Instead he studied Scott and her for a moment before he exhaled and nodded. "Why not? We can always squeeze one more passenger in. I'll tell the pilot you're on special assignment with the sheriff's office to watch over an officer."

Minutes later, she followed Scott's gurney as the

EMTs pushed it toward the helicopter. She turned and looked back at Scott's family gathered at the edge of the landing area. Kate waved and cupped her hands around her mouth. "We'll be over on the first ferry in the morning, and we'll bring you some clothes."

"Thanks," Lisa yelled back.

Her graze drifted over Kate and Brock, Betsy and Emma, who waved and threw kisses toward the helicopter. Their search for a lost brother had ended in a united happy family. But her search had uncovered a brother whose only desire was to see her dead.

The thought pierced her heart for a moment until she looked back at the family who would also soon be hers. God had taught her a great lesson today. *Sometimes the things we desire aren't what is best for us. In His love for us, though, He places great blessings around us that we can't see because we're too busy looking in the wrong places.*

God had opened her eyes to what He wanted for her, and she wasn't going to dwell on the past anymore. She turned and waved to her soon-to-be family and climbed into the helicopter next to Scott.

Six weeks later Lisa pulled her new car to a stop in the parking lot of the Green Hills Nursing and Rehabilitation Center in Durham. She switched the motor off and slid her hand across the car seat. Scott wrapped his fingers around hers.

She smiled and glanced at the redbrick building where her father lived. For a long time she'd dreamed of the day they would meet. Now that it was here, all she could think about was how thankful she was to have Scott beside her. For two weeks after the shooting she, Kate and Betsy had taken turns sitting by his bedside. Finally, his doctors had declared him out of danger and allowed him to return home.

He smiled, and she offered up another quick prayer of thanks for his recovery. "What is it?" he asked.

"I'm just so happy you're well."

He chuckled and squeezed her hand. "I had to get better. I was about to suffocate with all the women in my family standing over me all the time." His smile faded, and he glanced at the nursing center. "Are you sure you want to do this?"

"Yes. I want to see my father. He won't know me, but that doesn't matter. Now that the DNA results are back, I know for sure Miles Fleming is my father."

Scott reached for her hand. "I just don't want you to be hurt."

"After everything's that happened, I don't think anything else concerning my father could hurt me. I can't judge him for choosing his son over my mother and me. He may have suffered from that decision more than I can ever know."

Scott pulled her hand to his mouth and kissed her fingers. "You've told me you've forgiven him, but what about Travis? How do you feel about him?"

She sighed and stared out the windshield. "I think about how different it was with your sisters. They wanted to find you and searched until they did. My brother passed me on the streets of Ocracoke all the time and knew who I was. He only cared about the money. I'm glad he survived to face the charges against him."

"Me, too. The evidence against him for Jeff's murder is strong. The bullets from the gun he shot me with match those that killed Jeff, and there's his confession to you. Plus there's the matter of your mother's murder, Wayne's death and Travis's suspected involvement in that park ranger's boating accident. His money won't keep him from going to prison for the rest of his life."

Lisa shook her head. "No, it won't. The sad thing is, though, that he was filled with hate for no reason. I wouldn't have tried to get any of his money."

"What's going to happen with Fleming Enterprises now?"

She shrugged. "I have no idea. Travis's lawyers didn't waste any time letting me know that since

I had never been recognized as a legitimate heir, I had no claim to any of the company's holdings." She grinned at him. "With my father incapable of claiming me now, I guess you won't get a rich wife after all. I need a husband to support me."

He put his hand on the back of her head, pulled her close and covered her lips with his. When he released her, he smiled. "I can't think of anything I'd like better."

Lisa caressed his cheek and turned to stare at the nursing center. She took a deep breath. "If you're not up to walking that far, I'll go in alone."

"I'm fine, Lisa. I want to be with you when you see your father."

They climbed from the car and walked hand in hand into the building. A receptionist sat at a desk behind a window in the reception area. She glanced up and smiled. "May I help you?"

"I called earlier about visiting Miles Fleming. Can you tell me what room he's in?" Lisa asked.

The woman ran her finger down a list of names and glanced up. "He's in 318, straight down the hallway. I told his nurse he was going to have company today, so you can check with her at the nurses' station in the hallway. Her name is Mrs. Wagner."

Lisa's heart hammered as she and Scott approached the nurses' station halfway down the hall. A woman wearing a name tag that identified her as Lora Wagner, RN, glanced up from studying a chart when they stopped. "May I help you?"

"We're here to see Miles Fleming. Can you tell me how he is today?"

The woman laid the chart on the desk and smiled. "He's been more responsive today than any other one lately. I'm glad you're here to visit on a good day. I must say I'm surprised, though."

Lisa frowned. "Why?"

"I don't remember him having another visitor in all the time he's been here. His son calls every once in a while, but he doesn't visit."

Lisa glanced at Scott. "That doesn't surprise me," he said.

Nurse Wagner stepped out from behind the desk. "I'll show you to his room."

Panic filled Lisa at the thought of seeing her father, and she turned to Scott. "I'm glad you're with me."

"I'll always be with you." He took her hand and led her forward.

Her father sat in a chair next to the single window in the room. He didn't resemble the man she'd seen striding down the streets of Ocracoke Village when she was growing up. This person bore no resemblance to that athletic individual.

A wizened old man with white hair clutched at the blanket covering his lap. Nurse Wagner touched his arm. "Mr. Fleming, you have visitors."

He turned from staring out the window and looked at the nurse. She backed away. "If you need me, push the call button beside the bed."

Lisa waited until the nurse had left before she stepped forward and knelt beside his chair. She took one of his hands in hers and stroked the wrinkled skin. "I wanted to see you," she whispered.

He didn't respond for a moment, but then he looked down at her. His forehead wrinkled, and he tilted his head to one side. His lips trembled, and he lifted his other hand from his lap and touched her cheek. "Roxanne?" The hoarse sound ground from his throat.

Lisa shook her head. "No, I'm not Roxanne. I'm her daughter...Lisa."

"Lisa?" His eyebrows arched, and he sank back in his chair. His mouth curled into a smile. "Lisa is a pretty girl."

The words tumbled from his mouth in the same singsong voice that had haunted her dreams for years. She was right. Someone had crooned those words to her when she was a little girl, and it had been Miles Fleming, her father.

"Oh, Scott," she cried. "He remembers me." Even as she said it, the momentary return of reason vanished and once again Miles Fleming retreated into the recesses of his mind. Lisa leaned over and kissed his cheek. "I'm glad I came today, and I'll be back to see you again. Maybe next time

I can tell you about my new life. All you have to do is listen."

She pushed to her feet, and Scott put his arm around her. "Are you ready to go?"

"Yes."

Neither spoke until they stopped on the front porch of the facility. Scott took her by the shoulders and turned her to face him. "Are you sure you're all right?"

As Lisa reached up to touch his cheek, the diamond ring on her left hand sparkled in the sunlight and reminded her how blessed she was. Scott was different from the other men she'd known. All of them had either abandoned or betrayed her and left her scared to trust again. But God had healed the wounds of the past and given her a wonderful man to love. Now a whole new life awaited her.

She wrapped her arms around his neck and pulled his head down until their lips almost touched. "I've never been better in my life."

* * * * *

Dear Reader,

I hope you enjoyed Scott and Lisa's story. I was particularly drawn to these characters, because I know so many people whose lives have been affected from things that have happened to them in the past.

Although we all suffer hurts and disappointments in life, God stands ready to replace those emotions with a peace that only He can give. Scott knew that, but it took him a long time to release the past and let God deal in his life.

If your life is ruled by the past, I would encourage you to read the Bible verse in the front of this book. The phrase, "for my strength is made perfect in weakness," gives us the assurance that God's love can overpower our doubts and fears. As new creatures in Christ, we can be free to live the life God wants for us.

I pray you can find that peace in your life.

Sandra Robbins

Questions for Discussion

1. Scott couldn't forgive his aunt for keeping him from his family for years. Have you ever felt betrayed by a family member? How did you deal with it?

2. Lisa never knew her parents and wondered what they were like. Do you have unanswered questions about past events that affected your life? Have you attempted to find the answers that have evaded you?

3. Scott was fortunate to find three sisters he didn't know existed and treasured his new family. Do you take time to tell your family how important they are to you and how much you love them?

4. When Lisa's house was ransacked, she became frightened. Have you ever been the victim of a home robbery or vandalism of your property? How did you react?

5. Scott came home from the military as an emotionally-wounded veteran. Do you know men or women who suffer from post-traumatic stress disorder? How do you minister to them?

6. The man Lisa thought she loved in the past turned out to be a criminal who used her. Have you ever misplaced your trust in another person?

7. Scott agonized over his failure to save those he saw die in battle, and it caused him to feel unworthy of anyone's love. Have you had experiences that made you feel undeserving of love? If not, have you ever known anyone who has?

8. In Lisa's search for answers about her family, she encountered more than she expected. Have you ever discovered truths about family members or friends you wished you didn't know? How did it affect your relationship with them?

9. Scott was willing to risk his life to save Lisa. Would you be willing to give your life for someone you loved? Would you be willing to place yourself in danger to help a stranger?

10. Lisa's search for family revealed a father suffering from Alzheimer's. Has anyone in your family been stricken with this disease? How do you cope with the health problems of those you love?

11. Lisa was able to forgive those who had taken so much from her life. Are you able to forgive

people who have wronged you? What does the Bible teach about forgiveness?

12. God reminded Scott of a great truth when he encountered a herd of sheep on a dusty desert road. Do you know the One who gave His life for you?

LARGER-PRINT BOOKS!

GET 2 FREE
LARGER-PRINT NOVELS
PLUS 2 FREE
MYSTERY GIFTS

Love Inspired®
SUSPENSE
RIVETING INSPIRATIONAL ROMANCE

Larger-print novels are now available...

LISUSLP11B

LARGER-PRINT BOOKS!

**GET 2 FREE
LARGER-PRINT NOVELS
PLUS 2 FREE
MYSTERY GIFTS**

Love Inspired

Larger-print novels are now available...

YES! Please send me 2 FREE LARGER-PRINT Love Inspired® novels and my 2 FREE mystery gifts (gifts are worth about $10). After receiving them, if I don't wish to receive any more books, I can return the shipping statement marked "cancel". If I don't cancel, I will receive 6 brand-new novels every month and be billed just $4.99 per book in the U.S. or $5.49 per book in Canada. That's a saving of at least 23% off the cover price. It's quite a bargain! Shipping and handling is just 50¢ per book in the U.S. and 75¢ per book in Canada.* I understand that accepting the 2 free books and gifts places me under no obligation to buy anything. I can always return a shipment and cancel at any time. Even if I never buy another book, the two free books and gifts are mine to keep forever.

122/322 IDN FEG3

Name	(PLEASE PRINT)

Address	Apt. #

City	State/Prov.	Zip/Postal Code

Signature (if under 18, a parent or guardian must sign)

Mail to the **Reader Service**:
IN U.S.A.: P.O. Box 1867, Buffalo, NY 14240-1867
IN CANADA: P.O. Box 609, Fort Erie, Ontario L2A 5X3

Not valid to current subscribers to Love Inspired Larger-Print books.

**Are you a current subscriber to Love Inspired books
and want to receive the larger-print edition?
Call 1-800-873-8635 or visit www.ReaderService.com.**

* Terms and prices subject to change without notice. Prices do not include applicable taxes. Sales tax applicable in N.Y. Canadian residents will be charged applicable taxes. Offer not valid in Quebec. This offer is limited to one order per household. All orders subject to credit approval. Credit or debit balances in a customer's account(s) may be offset by any other outstanding balance owed by or to the customer. Please allow 4 to 6 weeks for delivery. Offer available while quantities last.

Your Privacy—The Reader Service is committed to protecting your privacy. Our Privacy Policy is available online at www.ReaderService.com or upon request from the Reader Service.

We make a portion of our mailing list available to reputable third parties that offer products we believe may interest you. If you prefer that we not exchange your name with third parties, or if you wish to clarify or modify your communication preferences, please visit us at www.ReaderService.com/consumerschoice or write to us at Reader Service Preference Service, P.O. Box 9062, Buffalo, NY 14269. Include your complete name and address.

LILP11B